The Fire Keeper's Girls

The Fire Keeper's Girls

L P Hansen

ONEPOTO PRESS

This story is a work of fiction. Names, characters, businesses, places, events and incidents are either the products of the author's imagination or used in a fictitious manner.

The brief biographies at the end of the book are based on material freely available in the public domain, and as accurate as the author is able to establish. The image of Chokyi Dronma is re-printed with permission from Columbia University Press. All other images are re-printed courtesy of Wikipedia and Wikimedia Commons on advice received from wikimedia.org.au.

ISBN 978-0-473-44472-3

Wellington, New Zealand

ONEPOTO PRESS

P O Box 52037

Titahi Bay

PORIRUA 5022

info@onepotopress.com

Contents

PART ONE

1

GEMMA

'I'm not going!' Gemma huddled in her bed, duvet pulled to her chin. 'You can't make me. What are you doing in my room anyway?'

'You must have heard the car and known we were home, Gemma. We waited for you to come down.' Her mother, as cool as ever. 'When you didn't hear me call, we decided to come up and give you the good news. A summer at the beach, isn't it exciting?'

Gemma gripped her sketchbook concealed under the covers, registering the roar of rush hour traffic, the familiar wail of a siren. 'You want me stuck in the country all summer? On my own, with a geriatric I hardly know?'

'Not on your own, Samantha's invited Alice too. You two were such friends when you were younger, when we saw more of your cousins. Poor Alice, it'll be nice for her.'

Gemma clenched her fists at a vivid flashback, not of Alice but of her three older brothers. Creeps. Alice might need a break, but spending the whole summer with her? 'No way. I've got plans and they don't include Alice.'

'You're going, Gemma,' Jane used her lawyer voice. 'Your father and I are working. You can't stay home alone, not as things are.'

Gemma pretended not to understand. 'I'm almost seventeen, I've done it before.'

'It's a condition of your – situation, Gemma. You know that perfectly well,' her mother snapped.

'I suppose you've told her –'

'Samantha's willing to have you, Gemma. Just be grateful. She's not even family.'

Her father then? Gemma turned to him. 'All that ultraviolet at the beach, Dad, d'you want me to die of skin cancer?'

'Sunlight might be good for you.' Henry forced a smile and reached to open her curtains.

Jane raised a hand to stop him. 'Gemma's room, Gemma's rules.' Her twittering laugh issued through taut lips. 'And our house, our rules. Dinner in ten minutes. We'll talk some more then.'

The smell of her mother's hairspray and perfume lingered after they left. Gemma pushed back her black curtains to open the window. Good old Henry, he meant well but if he smelt of anything it would be boring books and dullness. Why hadn't he stood up for her?

How could they send her to an old woman she'd met only once when she was a kid? She wouldn't stay. Maybe she could run away? Steal a car? She'd got money and could drive.

She opened her door, wrinkling her nose. Microwaved curry and rice. Again.

Gemma wheeled her case into the large transport centre, recoiling at the noise. She'd expected a couple of old-fashioned waiting rooms. Every exit looked the same and the place stank of cigarettes. Voices boomed from speakers and uniformed staff lounged everywhere, ignoring the crowds. She hated it.

On the train, with an empty seat beside her she'd been able to draw – but this? She turned in a panicky circle, scrutinizing the four ways out of the building.

'Gemma? Over here.'

Gemma spun around to see her cousin Alice waiting by a bench with a suitcase. An Alice grown taller – and bigger. Her neck now hid behind wobbly chins and under her shapeless summer dress, a sizeable roll trembled where once her waist had been. Only her beautiful eyes were the same, observing Gemma as she approached. She made no move to greet her.

'Hi, I forgot where we were supposed to meet. Good trip?' Gemma avoided looking at her.

'Long and hot on the bus, but okay. You?' Alice sounded wary.

'Not bad.' Was this it, for the whole summer? Should she make a dash for it, get another train? Go – anywhere?

Too late. Samantha, tall and straight, her long red hair streaked with grey, swept in to collect them. A few more wrinkles but Gemma recognised her at once. She wore some sort of flowing garment with a matching scarf tied around her hair. Several people turned to look.

'Gemma and Alice, welcome. I'm Samantha, some people call me Sam. Luggage okay? Got everything? Let's get out of this madhouse.' The same voice, firm and clear. She led them to the car park where a scarlet Range Rover convertible waited. Impressive, even with the roof up.

As they heaved cases into the rear, Samantha caught Gemma's look. 'Want the hood down?' And so they travelled away in style, with the sun on their faces and hair flying in the wind.

Gemma clutched at her seat as Samantha spun the vehicle through town, accelerating through traffic lights turning red and narrowly missing several flowerbeds. When they reached the open road, Gemma unclenched her grip and sank back. Poor Alice in the back, she'd have got the worst of it.

'The place has grown since you were here last,' Samantha shouted to Gemma over the noise of the engine. 'On the whole I like it, just not the traffic.'

The town was so small. And this straight, narrow road, now taking them deep into grassland – as a child, Gemma had been terrified by its endless length and the emptiness all around. But she'd learned a lot since then, how to help herself to transport, for a start.

After driving for a time they crossed a bridge, then turned off the main road onto an unsealed lane. Samantha's home huddled in a remote bay, Gemma recalled, the only house around. How did people live that way?

When the big vehicle stopped, the silence dazed her. Without the engine noise and wind in her ears, it took several moments to catch the soft swish of waves, the rustle from large trees now protecting the house. She clambered out and stretched, the sun warming her chilled face. Blue water and blue sky to the horizon – and that little island out in the bay, she'd forgotten it. Before she could look around, Alice hauled their luggage from the wagon. Proper reconnaissance could come later.

They wheeled their cases into the front hall and left them there, as Samantha led them on a rapid tour of the house. Wooden floors, colourful rugs, curios and artworks passed in a blur as she hustled them from room to room. Through the windows, Gemma glimpsed more outbuildings than she remembered.

In the kitchen, Samantha poured drinks from a frosted jug. 'We'll be sharing this house for some time, so I've got some rules.' She handed round their glasses.

Oh great, more rules. Gemma sniffed her drink. It smelled lemony, she'd risk it.

'For the first week we do what we like, provided we don't bother each other,' Samantha sipped her juice. 'We'll mostly cook and eat together and I may ask for help, but not often.'

Okay so far, but there'll be a catch. Wait for it. Gemma drank some more.

'However it is my home, so here are the three rules,' Samantha counted them off on her fingers. 'Don't swim alone, that's number one. You're both excellent swimmers – I checked – and it's a safe beach, but it's selfish to get into trouble and spoil things for others. Two. Clean up after yourselves. Work out your own systems in your bedroom. You're sharing, but it's a big enough space to draw a line down the middle if you have to.'

Alice made a gurgling sound as she gulped at her drink.

'Did you have a question?' Samantha glanced at her but Alice shook her head, setting her chins quivering.

'Rule three, for the first week I want you to come with me on one outing every day and keep some sort of record of how you find it.' Samantha handed each of them a large notebook. 'In these, please.'

'Every day?' Gemma objected as she took the book.

'Every day. We begin tomorrow with a trip to a gypsy fair, leaving here at ten. We won't be there long.

That's all. You've got time to unpack before dinner.'

A gypsy fair didn't sound too bad, but a diary? Seriously weird. Gemma got her case and followed her uncommunicative cousin to their shared bedroom.

2

ALICE

Alice's mood lifted as she wheeled her case to their room. What an amazing place. Solitude – she rolled the word round in her mouth. Somewhere to swim, a private beach -- and only a few rules. And Samantha or Sam – she'd stay sharp round her. Alice knew this was no ordinary holiday. Still, an exhilarating ride through town, a comfortable house crammed with exotic things – and Gemma. Okay so far.

Gemma needed company, that's the story her mother gave her when the invitation came. From what she'd overheard, Alice knew otherwise.

Painfully thin, with her dyed black hair and kohl-blackened eyes, Gemma could have some terrible disease. But she'd also taken to face piercings and black clothing in a big way so maybe melodramas again? That's the Gemma Alice remembered.

Her own mother and Gemma's father kept in touch as sister and brother, but the families rarely got together any more. Had the novelty of having daughters born in the same month worn off? When everything changed? After Eric?

Gemma chose the bed facing the cliffs, leaving her the picture window overlooking the bay. Alice packed her clothes into the sweet-smelling chest of drawers on her side of the room, finding a sachet of real lavender at the back. She'd not only hear the sea but see it and the stars as well, if she didn't close the curtains. Bliss. She put her notebook on her pillow. She'd use her code to write about the outings, it kept out her brothers and would keep Sam out as well. Although a gypsy fair sounded harmless enough.

Gemma pulled her own clothes out of her case, stuffing them into an oak chest near her bed. Every item black.

Alice finally broke the silence. 'Everything okay at home? Your dad? How's Henry?'

Gemma shrugged. 'Climbing the legal ladder, trying to catch up to Jane, as usual. They're both fine, I guess,' she grimaced. 'And your mum? How's Tracey?'

'Slaving away for her boys, nothing's changed there.' Alice turned away as tears pricked her eyes. She kicked her empty case under the bed, then straightened up and tried again.

'Sam's okay, I thought she'd be different. I like the Range Rover and the house, and it's a great beach.' Would Gemma say it didn't compare to Acapulco or the south of France, places Alice could only dream of seeing? She braced herself, but Gemma just nodded and pulled on a black sweater.

They ate home-cooked lasagna in the living room, balancing trays on their knees and watching a comedy film on a giant screen. No need to talk – or even look at each other.

Alice noted the expensive sound system, artworks on the walls, couches strewn with colourful cushions, thick Oriental rugs on the floors. Whatever Sam did, it worked for her.

After the movie and tidying up from their meal, Alice slipped away for a walk. With the tide going out, her bare feet sank into wet sand. She meandered along the empty beach, enjoying the peace.

The tall cliffs and one rocky outcrop in particular caught her attention and she strolled towards it. Sedimentary, so there could be fossils? Paleozoic? Mesozoic? Cenozoic? She recited the words like a ritual. Their sonorous sounds brought back memories of her almost five-year old self, struggling to repeat them to her father. His pleasure at her efforts and her reward, his tales of plant collecting in far-off places.

But now that she'd mastered his language and begun to decipher its meanings, Eric wasn't here to share it with her. Where was he? Why couldn't they find him? The persistent questions swarmed in her mind like angry bees. 'Stop it!' Alice spoke aloud and dashed away a tear. 'You're here and he's not. Stay sharp.'

More significant was why they'd come to this place,

she and Gemma? Alice knew almost nothing about Sam, but overhearing Tracey's words on the phone to her brother were warning enough. 'You're sure Sam's game can fix them both?'

Her mother's guilty start as she came into the room gave her away. Alice dreaded yet more of Tracey's therapists and pretending she hadn't heard, hurried into the kitchen. When Tracey volunteered her story about Alice being company for Gemma at the beach, Alice didn't bother to argue. Almost anything was better than another holiday spent at home and she'd dealt with nosy do-gooders before. She'd manage.

Without fuss, not even the usual dramas about money, Alice found herself on her way to spend summer at the beach with Samantha, a woman she'd never met. A woman who could apparently 'fix them both?' She'd talk to her cousin, they needed to look out for each other.

A flock of sea birds flying inland showed white against the darkening sky and Alice watched them. Nothing else moved and she stood motionless, absorbed by the scene until a chill breeze led her to retrace her footsteps still showing deep in the sand.

Back at the house there was no sign of Gemma. Was that the shower running? Sam glanced up from a couch in the living room, and put down her book. 'Find your way alright?' she asked. 'As I said, it's quite safe. I think of it as my own beach. Apart from us here, there's no easy access except by sea, because of the cliffs.'

'It's lovely,' Alice said. She meant it. 'Thanks again for inviting me here with Gemma.' She watched for Sam's reaction. Stretched out in her colourful clothing, the older woman looked relaxed but Alice wasn't fooled. Sam missed nothing.

'My pleasure,' Sam said and returned to her book. 'Got everything you need?' she added, not looking up. 'Get a hot drink in the kitchen if you want one, you know where everything is.'

So innocuous, but the interrogations would start soon and Alice would be ready. In her room she wrote 'Arrival day' in code in the notebook, and noted down her observations so far.

3

GEMMA

Sitting beside Sam in the big vehicle the next morning, Gemma darted cautious glances at the controls. Could she handle it? What if something went wrong? No help around here.

Sam had the SUV's roof up this time so she could be heard. She pointed out surf beaches and tree-lined properties as they drove but Gemma ignored her, too busy counting side roads and intersections. After a time, Sam pressed a button and music filled the space. 'Café del Mar, chill-out choice,' she called to Alice in the back seat and Gemma caught the amusement in her voice. What was so funny?

Ten minutes later, Sam turned into a grassy field taking one of the few spaces left in the informal car park. Under the nearby trees, the semi-circle of caravans and tents already teemed with activity. Gemma smelt incense, popcorn, crushed grass, food cooking. Accordion music played from speakers and brightly dressed children shepherded people from one attraction to another.

'Let's meet a friend of mine.' Sam led them towards

a distinctive van, taller than the others and intricately decorated.

A black-haired girl arranging shawls on an outdoor table saw them coming and rapped a signal on the van's wall. The door opened and a small, brown-skinned old woman came down the steps, greeting Samantha with cries of delight. The two exchanged hugs and words in a strange language, then Sam introduced them.

'Yes, yes, my dears, I am Aishe. This is my granddaughter Lela. Come in, come in,' the old woman indicated the van.

Gemma followed them into a dazzling confusion of light and dark. Almost every part of the large van's dark interior was carved or mirrored. Surfaces reflected back bits of other things; parts of doors, objects and people showed in several places at once. She made her way to a colourful cushioned alcove and Alice joined her.

'My man, Guda, he loved to carve wood and play tricks.' Aishe's brown eyes creased into a smile as she watched them look around. 'Now I can no longer see him everywhere I look, I treasure my memories instead.' She held out her hands to them. 'So girls, you are with Samantha for a summer of the great Game. Are you ready?'

Alice's head jerked up and she nodded. When Aishe looked at her, Gemma nodded too – but what game? What were they talking about?

'You are brave girls. You'll come to no harm. Now, tell me what you know about gypsies. Can we foretell the future?' A sly grin. 'Don't be shy.'

Was she serious? Gemma kept quiet.

After an embarrassing silence Alice burst out, 'It's unlikely, or you'd have known the Nazis' plans for killing gypsies in the Second World War.'

Aishe drew in a sharp breath and gave Alice an appreciative look. 'So, we have a smart girl here. Tell me, Alice, why are we called travellers?'

Alice reddened but gestured around the van at the stacks of shawls. 'You travel for work?'

'A good answer, yes. We also keep our own language and customs. That makes people uneasy, so they move us on. Samantha knows some Romany words that I've taught her, but she enjoys everything exotic. And you?' She turned to Gemma. 'What do you know of gypsies?'

'Not much, just the music and dancing I've seen in films,' Gemma mumbled. The fabulous clothes too, but she wouldn't admit that.

'Yes, that traditional music, I adore it. Lela is completing her studies in music but for her it must always be classical. Such a clever girl,' Aishe beamed. 'All my family are educated now. In my time, we weren't welcome in schools, of course.'

Gemma fidgeted at this mention of bigotry that she knew nothing about.

Aishe turned to Sam and spoke in the strange

language. Their lowered voices and urgent tones suggested more than a chat.

Then Sam stood up, tucking the folded page Aishe had given her into her bag. 'Until next time,' she said, embracing the older woman. 'We'll look around the fair now. Don't forget to email me your travel plans. And keep me informed,' she added with emphasis.

Aishe indicated a laptop glowing on a shelf. 'I insist on education so my grandchildren insist on computers,' she chuckled. 'Enjoy yourselves, girls. We may meet again, before summer is over.'

Gemma couldn't get out of the van quickly enough, away from the spooky old woman with her piercing eyes and talk about being brave. She wanted to explore the stalls.

The lavish displays of crafts and jewellery, gifts and clothing didn't disappoint her. Sam seemed in no hurry and they browsed at leisure. When Alice admired an embroidered Boho smock, Sam insisted she try it on. The filmy emerald and scarlet fabric draped easily over her hips and Alice's gaze lingered on the garment as she handed it back.

'Shall we buy it?' Sam asked. 'You can choose one thing each today, I'll pay. Your families arranged an allowance.'

Eyes wide, Alice clutched the shiny bag as though she'd never before had such a gift. Perhaps she hadn't.

A nearby hat stall caught Gemma's attention. She'd never been a geeky sunhat person but the black fedora – if she tilted it over one eye? Once it was hers, she kept it on.

'Now you?' Alice asked Sam but she shook her head.

'I've more than enough clothes, I'll just look.'

When they were through exploring, they brought flatbreads stuffed with salad and cheese and munched on them as they returned to the car park.

Back at the villa with the tide high, both girls changed into swimming gear and headed for the beach

For day one, it hadn't gone too badly. Gemma floated on her back, looking at the sky. She hadn't met gypsies before and the fair wasn't too boring. A chance to check out the SUV and the roads too.

She rolled over. Alice floated nearby, her hands behind her head. They still hadn't talked much. 'You knew a lot about gypsies.'

'I read,' Alice said, lifting an eyebrow. 'I read and I think about what I read.' She tipped her head and glanced at Gemma. 'D'you know the Roma community, the gypsies, get fingerprinted in Italy? They're just assumed to be criminals. That's horrible.'

She raised herself so she could see the house. Paddling closer, she whispered to Gemma, 'Sam's gone inside but voices carry over water. Talk quietly. Why are you here?'

Gemma stared at her. 'I don't know,' she whispered back. 'Something to do for the holidays, I suppose. Henry's got a contract away from home and they won't leave me on my own.'

'Don't act dumb, there's more to it than that,' Alice scoffed, keeping her voice low. 'Our parents are up to something. I heard Tracey on the phone to your father about Sam sorting us out. It's something about a game.'

'That's what Aishe said,' Gemma frowned.

'Whatever it is, it's for people in trouble,' Alice persisted. 'So what's your problem?'

Gemma studied her. With her wet hair plastered to her round face, Alice looked more like the kid she remembered – but could she trust her?

'Maybe a few dramas at home,' she hedged. 'Why, what about you?'

'Maybe a few dramas?' Alice echoed. 'What do you think? Why else would someone finish up looking like this?' She gestured at her body. 'Yes, I've had a few dramas too. A lot of bad stuff went down, and then too many pills.' She waved away Gemma's shocked gasp. 'But I'm still here. Tracey brought in some freaks to sort me out.' Long pause. 'Fat people can't be intelligent so they treated me like a moron. It didn't go well.'

Her story struck Gemma as cold as a breaking wave. Not Alice, clever Alice?

'I think Sam's supposed to cure me over the summer, since they failed,' Alice went on, shaking water from her eyes. 'So what about you?'

She'd have to say something now, after that. 'I've dropped out a bit since you saw me last,' Gemma muttered, treading water. 'School's crap. A factory turning out clones, labourers for capitalism. I won't buy into it.'

Alice's scornful sniff said she didn't buy into her story either.

'Okay, I got mixed up with some people who're kind of – anarchists,' Gemma admitted. 'They finished up a bit crazy.' Was Alice with her so far? At a nod from her cousin, she stumbled on.

'They got into some – trouble. Someone was arrested and I was a key witness. There's been major fall-out. I've had exclusion from school, compulsory counselling. It's like prison at home now.'

'Then we're both candidates for rescuing,' was all Alice said. 'So what's Sam's game, d'you think? I don't trust her and you shouldn't either. We should stick together. There's something not right about this invitation.'

Sam, some sort of shrink? Gemma couldn't take it in. If Alice was right, she daren't run. But to stay here all summer, miles from anywhere? She shuddered.

By unspoken agreement, they swam back to the shore but something had shifted between them.

Sam called them to join her in the kitchen after they'd changed. 'Help me fix a meal,' she said. 'I've a cauliflower ready in the garden and it's best eaten fresh.'

Gemma eyed her cautiously. Was she a therapist? Her parents always spoke of Sam as a long-standing acquaintance, not a particularly close friend. If they had any. After one party, Jane had been scathing about Sam's clothes, she remembered, her voice tight with disapproval about some Chinese outfit with slits in the skirt. Henry just sounded amused. But had they said anything about her work? If so, Gemma had missed it.

Alice fetched and trimmed a large head of cauliflower from Sam's vegetable garden, evidently knowing how to prepare it. Gemma hadn't known they came with leaves, huge green things curling over the top. While the cauliflower steamed, her cousin made a complicated dressing that Sam admired.

Sam herself prepared pasta and grated several cheeses and at her prompting, Gemma put out plates and sliced bread from a loaf. At least she could do that. At Sam's suggestion, she also poured a glass of chilled white wine for each of them. The meal wasn't too bad, almost companionable with everyone drowsy after their day in the sun.

As they washed the dishes Alice said, 'Thanks for the Fair today, the lunch and my top.' She might have been speaking to a school principal. 'What's the plan for tomorrow?'

'It's tomorrow night,' Sam put a glass in the draining

rack. 'We'll take the boat over to the club on the island. A jazz group's visiting and I've got three tickets.'

Gemma winced. A whole night of old people's music?

Alice studied Sam, making no comment on the jazz. 'So, our notebooks? Will you want to look at them?'

'No, never.' Sam dropped a dish back in the sink and turned to Alice. 'Whatever gave you that idea? You might find some notes on your time here useful, that's all.'

'I bet,' Alice muttered as she stacked plates in the cupboard but only Gemma heard.

'I'll respect your privacy and you respect mine,' Sam added. 'I sometimes have friends call late in the evening and I don't expect to be disturbed.'

Something in her voice made Gemma look up. Not a man surely, at her age? Gross.

'There've been some security issues lately, so we need to lock up when we're away for long,' Sam changed the subject. 'I'll show you where the keys are kept. We close the windows when we're out too, the weather's changeable.'

The following day they swam, read and made themselves snacks when they were hungry. In the afternoon Gemma held a climbing bean frame steady while Sam repaired it and Alice busied herself in the small vegetable garden.

In the house later, Gemma eyed the landline telephone. It was torture having no Wi-Fi. Even worse, no cell phone coverage. She'd discovered that within minutes of arriving. Sam said they could use the old phone, but with others listening? No way! That was the genius of texting, sharp, private exchanges – a game in themselves. And this game that Alice was on about? No signs of anything so far, had she got it wrong?

After a light meal they got ready for the evening, Gemma keeping to her usual black, just adding the hat. Alice wore her Boho top over a skirt, while Samantha's strappy dress showed off her still-trim figure. Tonight she'd looped up her hair and an entire turquoise arm party sparkled under her embroidered shawl.

Gemma and Alice waited on the narrow wharf as Sam readied the small launch moored beside it. Painted white with a scarlet trim, it bore the name Apsara.

'It means Divine Dancer,' Sam interpreted Gemma's questioning glance as they climbed on board. She started the outboard motor and steered them towards the island. Too far to swim but worth checking out anyway if she needed to get away. Gemma hadn't been there before.

In spite of its name, the club was just a hall packed with people on folding chairs. As she located their seats, Sam greeted several friends but didn't introduce them. Gemma kept her head down, avoiding people's eyes.

The chattering crowd fell silent as the musicians,

an all-female coloured group, took their places. With a few chords for introduction, they filled the air with music, one harmony following another. Melancholy music interrupted by solos from each player, trombone, trumpet, saxophone, keyboard and drums. The audience clapped and stamped their feet after each solo, Gemma clapping too, caught up in the mood.

When the group paused for a break, the trombonist put down her instrument and moved forward to speak.

'Jazz was born as women gained the right to vote.' Her glance swept the room. 'With the men away at war, women were in the workplace and they were sassy. They stepped into the jazz clubs and played their hearts out.' The gravelly voice paused and the moment lengthened. 'African-American women sang for their lives; they had to. There were black women stars in the US music and movie industry who couldn't come in the front door to collect their awards. Couldn't use the bathrooms white folks used, couldn't sit at the same table.' Her dark eyes flashed. 'All that pain is in their music and I'm glad if it makes you sad. It should.' Her tone softened. 'But they kept going, and we stand on their shoulders today.'

As Gemma absorbed her words, the musicians hurled themselves into their next piece, a wild and restless riot of melody. Pouring your pain into something? Gemma knew about that. What an unlikely place to find others who did the same.

Slouched in the seat next to her, Alice stirred at a disturbance from the back of the room. Some young people pushed towards empty seats near the front. Talk about making an entrance. Couldn't they wait? But they'd broken the mood and not long afterwards, the show ended.

People around her grumbled and glanced at the newcomers.

'Locals,' Sam indicated with her shoulder. 'Want to stay for supper? Maybe meet them?'

Gemma shook her head and Alice did the same. 'We'll go then.'

After some brief farewells, she led them to the boat. Making no attempt at conversation, she trailed one hand in the phosphorescent water, humming as she steered them back to the wharf.

Gemma gazed up at the stars, her head full of rhythms.

'Food farm shopping tomorrow morning,' Sam told them as they walked up to the house. 'That's our outing. I'd like to leave right after breakfast, okay with you two? There'll be time for a swim afterwards.'

4

ALICE

'Have you written anything yet?' Alice scribbled in her notebook as she asked the question the next morning. A commotion from some sea birds had woken them both and she'd dressed, ready for the day.

Gemma pulled the sheets up to her chin. 'Nah, I figured I'd make something up at the last minute, in case Sam checks.'

'You'll only get long-term memories that way,' Alice stopped writing. 'The short-term ones are more intense, that's why I write things down straight away. We need all the information we can get. What's Sam's message with that jazz, d'you think?'

'Message?' Gemma stretched. 'She just wanted to hear some music and dragged us along.'

Was she that dim? 'You still haven't got it, have you?' Alice slammed down her pen. 'You think this is a holiday camp? We're being watched all the time, that's why I make notes. It's our one chance of figuring out what Sam's up to.'

'You're paranoid.' Gemma rolled over and burrowed down in her bed.

'And you're blind,' Alice retaliated. 'We're under surveillance, get used to it.'

Gemma sat up, yawning. 'Look, your brothers may hassle you at home but no one's out to get you here. So what if Sam's some sort of shrink? Just go along for the ride.'

Alice ticked items off on her fingers. 'We'd no choice about coming, either of us. Why ask us? It's not like she owes your parents any favours, and she doesn't even know Tracey or me. Why buy us those clothes? It's to soften us up. What about the outings? And even Aishe knew about this game that's supposed to straighten us out.'

'Sam would've told Aishe we were coming,' Gemma objected. 'They're friends. What's the big deal?'

'You used to have a brain.' Why wouldn't Gemma listen? 'Fried with drugs from your weird friends, is it?'

Gemma flung herself out of bed, fists clenched. 'Mind your own business, at least I've got friends.'

Alice whirled around and left the room. She stalked into the kitchen to find Sam making toast. Had she heard them arguing?

After breakfast, Alice dived for the back seat of the wagon. Let Gemma talk to Sam. She'd listen and make notes. She'd had plenty of practice managing on her own.

Sam drove them further into the countryside, then down a tree-lined avenue before parking under some linden trees. Walking through the landscaped grounds, Alice smelled the market before they reached it. Her irritation dissolved instantly in the scents of bread, spices and other fragrances.

Their path led to a large open-sided barn filled with stalls and surrounded by outbuildings, thronged with people. Sam smiled at her surprise. 'Welcome to the Food Farm. Let's look around, there's lots to see.'

She led them to a booth called the Mushroom Log. Alongside regular mushrooms, fairy-tale fungi in shades of cream and yellow emerged from wooden twigs and bunches of thin white stalks grew up from jars. Miniature brown fungi sprouted from small branches like tiny brown steps, while oyster mushrooms clung to suspended bags of – was that coffee grounds? Alice stared, inhaling the pungent odours, then read the information sheets.

'People eat these things?' She peered at the shapes. 'They look like something Alice in Wonderland would trip out on.'

Sam chuckled and the denim-clad stallholder offered them morsels on toothpicks. Closing her eyes Alice sniffed and then sampled the moist fragments. Woodsy, earthy, different textures, tender, firm, even chewy. She browsed the proffered recipe pages, tucking some into their bulging brown paper bags when they left. How could Gemma look so bored?

Sam guided them next to the Cheese Corner, a

strong-smelling booth with multi-coloured wheels and slices of not only golden cheeses but also orange, red and even black. Some were studded with seeds, others rolled in spices. Soft cheeses, hard cheeses, runny cheeses with unpronounceable names, presided over by an artisan cheese maker with a belly as round as his products.

He showed Alice how to sniff and press cheeses for firmness, offered slivers so fine they melted on her tongue. Salty, creamy, spicy, some so pungent she hesitated to put them in her mouth, these were cheeses worthy of respect. Tiny water crackers cleaned their palates between samples, but Alice soon held back. When Gemma also declared herself full, Sam collected several wedges wrapped in waxed paper and they moved on to a larger booth, The Bread Basket.

There were fragrant black breads, brown and white breads, breads dotted with seeds and spices, twists, twirls and fruity rounds. Having glimpsed the stalls ahead of them, Alice tasted just a cube or two of darkest rye. After some discussion, Sam and Gemma selected a loaf each.

They strolled past olives, nuts and nut butters, oils, wines, eggs, cakes, pickles, preserves, herbs as well as stalls of regular fruit and vegetables. Sam's shopping included chats and sampling, giving Alice time to look around.

This was a Food Fiesta, not just a farmers' market.

She'd never seen anything like it. Nothing like supermarket shopping for the stodgy food her brothers demanded.

'These stall holders must like seeing their products appreciated,' she said to Sam.

'They value their regular customers,' Sam agreed. 'Who's the main cook in your household?'

'Mostly me, my brothers are always hungry.'

'And you?' Sam murmured, but Alice pretended not to hear.

5

GEMMA

Seeing Sam and Alice engrossed in food talk, Gemma retreated to a row of hay bale seats. Spending so much time with others and sharing a room – it was all getting to her. At least Alice didn't talk much, to her anyway.

Not that there were many conversations at home either, just instructions. Or arguments that Jane always won. Jane, the legal phenomenon, the woman who took just a few weeks off work for her daughter's birth. The woman who made partner in a big law firm before she was thirty. The woman who took it for granted that Gemma would be a lawyer too. Gemma sketched a judge's wig with tight curls in her notebook.

And Henry? Like an iceberg, Henry showed just a bit of himself above water. Gemma was sure he'd rather be in real estate than law. Why did he work as a lawyer, when the only bit he enjoyed was helping people buy and sell houses? Her official caregiver, Henry retreated to his home office as soon as Jane's high heels clicked out the front door each morning. The first words she learned were probably from the Do Not Disturb sign on his door.

A string of nannies and au pairs ferried her to and from early childcare and private schools with after-school programmes, until she was old enough to spend more time alone. Dodging boarding school was more about her mother's work as a family lawyer than her own welfare, but Gemma didn't care. Communal living would have been agony with no privacy to sketch.

She'd always drawn, created adventures for the crowd that peopled the world inside her head. Alone in her room, she filled sketchbook after sketchbook with their intricate lives. The stories changed but some characters remained, voicing her own thoughts and feelings. There were dangerous stories too, ones that no one must see. So her sketchbook stayed zipped inside the lining of her case on this holiday, any new stories staying in her head. Instead she made small sketches in Sam's dumb notebook. All morning, she'd drawn people sampling food and shopping.

After a dozen stalls, she'd been more than ready to carry everything back to the wagon. How much food did three people need? But Sam claimed it was cool enough under the trees to leave the shopping in its chiller bags. She wanted another look around and a stop at a café and Alice agreed. The food maybe? Yet she didn't snack or eat much at mealtimes.

So they'd checked out a cooking demonstration, kitchen tools and some lethal-looking knives. Gemma tagged along. Actual cooking was a waste of time, surely? At home, Gemma helped herself to convenience food from the kitchen freezer. Her mother ordered in everything they needed. Gemma didn't even recognise some of the fruits and vegetables, and as for gadgets like pasta makers and dumpling moulds?

Absently, she sketched Sam's tall frame as she leaned forward to listen to a stall keeper. Alice was right, Sam noticed everything. Did she suspect how alien Gemma found this world, with its gypsies and jazz, weird food and cooking? Alice must find it strange too but kept on talking, probably investigating. A new Alice with her secrets, her defiance over taking those pills. Gemma had heard a lot from Jane about clever Alice but nothing about pills.

Gemma let out a breath. Let Alice investigate, she'd draw – while she could. She pulled down the brim of her hat and studied the crowds.

That evening, Sam insisted they make dinner from their purchases, using a recipe Alice had brought back. Gemma found herself facing a heap of smelly mushrooms. Did you peel the things? Throw away the stalks? Sam took pity on her and passed over some garlic cloves instead, showing her how to crush them with the back of a knife until the papery skin peeled off easily. But the smell! Gemma took a break at the open kitchen door and stared out to sea, shutting out the sound of the others chopping vegetables together and chatting.

An exasperated shout from Sam brought her back into the room. 'Gemma!' Sam thumped her knife on the bench. 'Alice tells me she's never been to the theatre or seen a live play. Please tell me you have.'

At Gemma's shrug and shake of her head, Sam sank onto a kitchen stool. 'But what about school?' she demanded. 'Surely you have drama classes? Don't you put on shows? Or is *all* your education online now? Do teachers still take their classes to the theatre?'

Alice said her school had outings to sports and cultural events but plays were something they read, occasionally.

'My curriculum's supposed to prepare me for law,' Gemma mumbled. 'Not drama. My parents never go to the theatre. Lawyers deal with real-life dramas every day of their lives, that's what Jane says. So why would they take me?'

'No shows, ever?' Sam probed.

Gemma confessed she'd once been in a school show. Jane and Henry kept their school visits for academic events so their Belgian au pair took her, praised her performance, said she was *talentvol*.

'Did you enjoy it?' Sam asked. Gemma admitted she'd liked her costume. A stab of memory brought back her fascination with the lighting and set design.

'Tracey couldn't afford to take us all to the theatre,' Alice said. 'I doubt she'd want to. The boys download movies and that's what she watches.'

'When the arts fall off the school curriculum, the future is bleak,' Sam grumbled. 'We get what we deserve, another nation of shopkeepers.'

The next morning at breakfast Sam waved some pages around, clearly pleased with herself. 'Tonight, we fill a gap in your education.' She showed them to Alice beside her. 'We're going to see a play, it's had rave reviews. It's a long drive up the coast to this theatre, but it'll be worth it.'

'By a young London playwright known for her incisive observations of society,' Alice read out. 'I bet that means she's taking a swipe at everything. There's even an age warning; Some content may offend. Are you sure it's *suitable* for us? '

Gemma registered her sarcasm – so much for the two of them bonding over food.

'It's been a sell-out in London's West End.' Sam retrieved the pages. 'I want to see it myself. After tonight's performance, they'll show a film clip of the author speaking to one of her London audiences.' She looked over her spectacles at Gemma and then Alice. 'Let's decide what to wear.'

While Gemma and Alice cleared the breakfast things Sam disappeared into her room, returning with her arms full of fabrics. She draped the items, mostly shawls, wraps and colourful scarves, across the table one by one.

'Dressing for the theatre's essential, it adds to the experience,' she smoothed the shawls. Most were in autumn tones. 'My colours,' she admitted. 'Not right for you two.' She held up a pashmina in magenta and green. Gemma fingered its soft folds. 'No, too warm for tonight,' Sam put it aside.

A deep turquoise triangle followed, heavily fringed and glistening like polished jade. 'Alice, this would match your new top. It's Chinese silk. Try it on.' Alice fingered the fringe as Sam draped it around her shoulders. 'Like it? Excellent, it's yours for tonight. Now Gemma, black or –?'

A stream of scarlet slid through her hands. Gemma gasped. Richly textured with flashes of orange, it was gorgeous.

'It's Spanish,' Sam eyed her critically as she looped it round her. 'It'll be perfect with your hat.'

'I can wear my hat to this play?' Gemma adjusted the silky wrap.

'Theatre-going clothes must be a feast for the eye,' Sam said. 'It's the very least an audience can do, offer tribute to all the work that goes into staging a production. Do you need anything else? No? You'll both look great. I'll do my best to match you.'

Gemma adjusted her hat as they waited for Sam that evening. 'Your shawl looks good,' she said to Alice.

But Alice wasn't listening. Her attention was riveted on the golden dragon that writhed down the front of Sam's black gown. Gemma gaped as the older woman strode in, a length of gold chiffon over her arm. A bright beaded contraption held her hair high and with her heels, she looked heroically tall. 'Ready?' she asked.

Oh Jane, if you could see us now. Gemma kept a straight face with difficulty and prepared to leave.

As Sam had said, it was a long drive to the theatre and on the way she entertained them with stories of plays she'd seen, actors she'd known. Arriving in the small seaside town at last, they found a park in a side street and walked to the theatre, joining others obviously going the same way. A river of people, dressed in their finery; Gemma eyed them curiously.

Flanked by modern shops and office buildings, the ornate theatre looked distinctly out of place. The crowd milled about, talking and greeting friends.

'We collect our tickets from the box office,' Sam joined a queue in front of a gilded kiosk inside the first door.

'Why's it called a box office?' Typical Alice, always asking questions.

'From Elizabethan days, when wealthy people sat on box seats in balconies.'

'And the poor stood?'

'You've got it.' Sam scooped up their tickets and

programme and steered them towards the stairs. 'Our seats are in the first gallery.'

Wide, carpeted stairs curved upwards out of sight. Gemma smoothed the dark, carved handrail as she followed Sam. She inhaled the musky scents of aged wood, perfume, flowers. Marble carvings gleamed from niches. Tall electric candlesticks glowed, lighting their way. Gilt and glamour everywhere.

They reached two massive doors, standing open. Beyond them Gemma saw row after row of tiered blue seats, curving upwards in a semi-circle to another balcony below an ornate plaster ceiling. Below their own balcony railing, she glimpsed yet more seats stretching forward to what must be the stage, unseen behind immense blue curtains.

'Wake up.' Alice nudged her as a white-shirted usher indicated their seats. Gemma moved as though in a trance. She sat. Stared. Soaked up the vibe, the buzz of the crowd, the electric atmosphere. How many people had sat here before her? Who had walked on that hidden stage over the years? Would she hear their voices if she listened beyond – beyond what?

'How old is this theatre?' Alice asked.

'A hundred years, or thereabouts,' Sam answered. 'Baroque theatres like this are rare. Plays are often staged in basements or halls. Even outdoors.'

'This place is huge,' Gemma found her voice. 'And so many people here.'

'With a show like this, they'll fill it almost every night and twice on Sundays, for a few weeks at least.' Sam adjusted her wrap.

Gemma shook her head in amazement, and then stiffened. Something was happening, she could feel it. The lights dimmed. The entire crowd hushed. Blackness. Silence. She held her breath. Music drifted up from invisible musicians somewhere far below her and then the huge curtains slid back.

Travelling home hours later along the dark country roads, Gemma hugged her knees to her chest, the red shawl discarded beside her. Her whole body was still too hot to wear it, even her fingers tingled! The play, so intense and angry had burned itself right into her. Raw emotion, openly exposed – yet being celebrated? Even praised?

Like the rest of the audience she'd been transfixed by the script and acting – but to have that glimpse of the author as well, what a bonus. The fierce energy of the woman, she knew that feeling, poured it into her own drawings.

She'd dived for the back seat after the show so she didn't have to talk, so she could relive the play, the theatre, every moment of the evening.

The story explored the catastrophic failure of parenting in a wealthy family. The father, absent abroad and the mother, assumed to be binge drinking at her club were never seen. The entire play featured the children aged seven to fourteen years, left to their own chaotic devices in their home, trapped in growing anxiety. As the play unfolded, they waited for days for a phone call from at least one parent that never came, knowing if they asked for help and their dilemma was discovered, they'd be split up and taken into welfare care.

As the young actors struggled to hold their world together, Gemma sensed others around her wiping away tears. Yet this interaction between the writer and her audience left her exultant. What an outlet for protest, show after show, every performance fresh and alive. Reaching new people every time.

She wanted to shout aloud at the marvels that playwriting offered an artist. Wilder than making up stories no one saw. More potent than spraying slogans on walls. Theatre was her world, she knew it. She belonged there.

Gemma exhaled, remembering the spiky, young playwright. Women are theatre's main audience, she'd said. Yet just ten percent of plays that get staged are female-authored.

'It's not because we can't write. Hundreds of trained playwrights compete for the few spaces allowed for females. But I'm an angry young woman. You'll be hearing more from me,' she'd said. Both her filmed audience and the live audience, Gemma amongst them, rose to their feet and cheered. Had she found her tribe?

For the first time, Gemma wrote in her notebook when she got into bed that night.

'The week's half over already,' Alice noticed her energetic scribbling. 'Are you catching up or just about tonight?'

'Tonight?' Gemma forgot her resolve to stay silent. 'It was magic! The theatre, the actors, everything. I didn't know there were plays like that. We read a bit of Shakespeare at school, but nothing like tonight.'

'I suppose there are families like that, where the kids stick together?' Alice's wistful tone made Gemma look up. Alice avoided her eyes and made a show of hanging up her top and smoothing out the colourful folds. 'A bit far-fetched, the play, but quite good acting.'

'Good? It was bloody brilliant,' Gemma burst out again. 'That play's the best thing I've seen in my life. I'd go again and again if I could. I'd see it a hundred times. I'd –'

Alice stared at her. 'Why don't you tell Sam you liked it,' she murmured. 'I think she'd be pleased to hear. You've haven't said much about the outings so far.'

Gemma stared back. 'What's got into you? Isn't Sam softening us up for her own sinister ends?'

Alice reddened. 'She's been pretty decent so far,' she admitted. 'Leaves us alone. I liked the Food Farm.'

She got into bed and closed her eyes.

Gemma's mind returned to their evening, to the mysterious moment when the curtains opened and the audience surrendered, willing hostages to the world in front of them. She reconstructed scene after scene in her head until her drooping eyes forced her into sleep.

6

ALICE

Okay, so Gemma was finally talking. She hadn't stopped babbling since she woke up. Her obsession with last night's play already irritated Alice and Sam's appreciative responses annoyed her even more. Why had she suggested Gemma speak to Sam in the first place?

Glaring at the two heads bent over the programme, Alice stomped into the garden, savouring a spurt of jealousy. Now Gemma had been suckered into Sam's web, she'd be even more useless. Why had Sam taken them to that dumb play? She hadn't said if she'd enjoyed it and the tickets were expensive.

Scowling, Alice recalled Sam's casual aside about an allowance. Her own mother wouldn't have put up much cash, she knew that. The whole money situation didn't add up. The fair, food farm and jazz were Sam's regular haunts so she took them along. But why the clothes? And then the play?

Alice sank into a garden chair. Nothing made sense. Had she misheard Tracey's words on the phone to Uncle Henry about a game to fix them? So far there'd been no well-meant advice from Sam, no earnest talks, no helpful books pushed at them.

She gave up and let the peace of the morning wash over her. Maybe she dozed, because next thing Gemma was shaking her. 'Sam says it's time to get your sandals on,' she grinned. 'For a mystery outing, leaving in an hour.'

They packed a picnic and drove inland, stopping by a remote lake. A rocky island in the centre of the dark water housed an oddly shaped building. A raised roof and domed crown at one end of the large structure suggested an observatory.

'It's a university research centre,' Sam explained, 'Mostly for earth sciences. Care to visit?' she teased.

'Really? We can go there?' Alice would swim if she had to.

They were to see an exhibition from the NEMO Science Center in Amsterdam, Sam said. She'd got them special access.

Alice stared across the water. She knew observatories needed remote locations with clear skies – but on an island? Miles from anywhere?

'Spooky,' Gemma shivered. 'Not for me, working out here with no one else around.'

'I doubt they even notice,' Sam laughed.

A small motor launch headed towards them, stirring the surface of the lake. They waited with their bags and picnic basket by the locked landing stage gate. The taciturn driver let them through without comment, saw them seated and turned the craft back to the island.

In the building's main entrance a tall, bearded man waited. After embracing Sam with lingering kisses on both cheeks, he introduced himself to the cousins as Mikael.

'I look after the Exhibitions we produce here,' he said. 'You two are what I need, intelligent young women to check out our new show.'

After stowing their bags and basket in a locker, he explained some more. 'This country needs more students interested in science, particularly girls. The Dutch have a way of making it relevant to students and they've lent us this show. We've a team reviewing the exhibits before they tour the regions after the summer.' He turned to Sam. 'Just let me have a word with Samantha, then we'll go and see it.' They hurried into a nearby office and closed the door.

Alice read signs leading to the Nanobiotechnology Core Facility, the Multimodal and Functional Imaging Laboratory, the Proteomics Core Facility? What were these places? Gemma browsed some leaflets and quickly replaced them. 'Might as well be in Polish,' she grimaced. 'I can't understand a word.'

After a few moments, Mikael opened the door and he and Sam set off down a corridor with Alice and Gemma hurrying after them. Rounding a corner, he ushered them into a spacious hall, crammed with exhibits and proceeded to guide them around the show.

And what a show. The exhibits showed science in a way Alice never dreamed possible. Colourful displays tempted her to touch, experiment, to play with the science of music, then genetics, climate change and more. Different experiments brought new discoveries. They pressed buttons, turned switches, even investigated the chemistry and biology behind teenage hormones. Mesmerised, Alice discovered more features each time she looked.

'All aimed at attracting your age group into science,' Mikael said. 'It works?'

'Yes!' Alice begged to go round again. She lingered by each item, questions pouring out of her. 'Who comes up with such ideas?'

'The Amsterdam science museum has five floors,' Mikael told her. 'You can see it online. But I think this will be enough for our travelling roadshow. We plan to develop exhibits like this.'

Alice slid her fingers through a gleaming DNA helix. 'I'd give anything to be part of that.'

'Then it's already doing its work,' he beamed.

After their second circuit ended, Sam paused. 'Mikael has work to do, it's time we left,' she said, lingering all the same.

Reluctant to leave the exhibition, or him? Alice hadn't missed the spark between them.

As they left the building promising more feedback, Alice exclaimed to Sam, 'Thank you, thank you. That's the best thing I've ever seen. What made you think of it?'

'Gemma told me about your pressed leaf collections from when you were little and suggested a science trip. I remembered this exhibition and I – called in some favours.' Sam headed towards the small wharf. 'We'll eat here, the launch skipper's still at his lunch.'

Alice's eyes filled with tears at the memory of those painstaking efforts to impress her father. And Gemma remembered? Mumbling thanks to her cousin, she helped unpack the food.

While they ate, Gemma showed her sketches of the show, some featuring their guide. 'Nice-looking,' she observed. 'An old friend, is he?'

'Not so old,' Sam's dry voice gave nothing away but Alice caught her slight smile. 'So Alice, you enjoyed yourself?'

'You know I did. We all did. How did you get us in there?'

'Perhaps it's best you don't know – but I'm glad you're fired up.'

Alice recalled the exhibits, detail by detail. Everything unpredictable, no 'right' or 'wrong'. True science was about theories, so this approach was perfect. Using teenagers' curiosity – just to see what happened. Even encouraging cooperation. Yet wasn't it impossible for scientists to share research freely? Governments demanded science make money. If it didn't turn a profit, was their research even funded?

Alice's online searches for her absent father had never turned up anything new from his botanical work. No new publications, no discoveries. So had it been worth it, abandoning his family? Why had he done it? Alice still dreamed of finding him, of asking him face to face.

7

GEMMA

Suggesting a science trip was one thing but for Sam to score a whole show for them? And a show crazy enough to make Alice drop her detective act, start raving on about trees and seaweed being the lungs of the planet? Gemma had never seen her look so alive. She'd be worth sketching.

Still high on a tide of goodwill after their night at the play, Gemma congratulated herself that Alice finally had something decent in her life. How did you live with your dad walking out on you? Gemma remembered almost nothing about her uncle Eric. Tall, thin and quiet, he'd travelled a lot – and then not come home. That was all she knew.

Tracey refused to speak about it. No photos of him existed in their home. Even her parents had taken down a family shot with him in it. Out of tact, or on Tracey's orders? Gemma knew she'd forbidden the kids to even use his name.

Alice never mentioned him, but Gemma still remembered her slaving over those leaf collections to show him when he came back from his latest trip.

Except that he hadn't. Twelve years later still no one knew where he was, although his employers and Tracey's lawyers had tried to find him.

Alice was turning out okay, quite good company really. Gemma was even learning a bit about cooking just by watching her. And it took the pressure off being with Sam when Alice did the talking for them both.

In their room that evening, she suggested they guess what outing Sam would come up with next. 'Whoever gets closest is let off dishwashing –' She pulled out her notebook. Their ideas ranged from scuba diving to a Japanese tea ceremony. They'd a lot to talk about, especially Sam.

'She can't be a therapist,' Gemma insisted. 'No lectures, no instructions. Just these amazing trips and no hassles afterwards.'

'She's generous,' Alice admitted. 'And she knows a lot of people. Today was spectacular.' Her voice trailed away.

'So was the play. I'm going to work in theatre if I have to run away to do it,' Gemma pleated the bed sheet between her fingers. 'I never wanted to do law. And you?'

Alice lay with her hands under her head, looking out the window. 'I've always wanted to work in botany but there's no money,'

'What about your brothers? Aren't they studying?'

'They have study funds that Dad set up, but he

disappeared before –' Alice broke off.

Before he got to you? Gemma silently finished for her. For Alice to mention her father, something must have shaken loose. 'You'll win a scholarship, you're so smart.' She kept her voice cheerful. 'Are you really up for years of lectures and assignments?'

'Botany's in my bones, I'd jump at the chance, especially after today.'

'Sam might think of something,' Gemma said. Alice's voice trailed off and she slept, but Gemma lay sleepless, creating stories in her head.

The next morning Sam ignored their bleary expressions and hustled them through breakfast. 'With all these trips, a tidy-up's overdue,' she declared. 'I'll put on some music to get us through it.'

Gemma was enjoying the mild disorder but Alice was keen to get started. 'Our place is always cluttered, half eaten pizzas and empty drink cans everywhere,' she confessed. 'Not like this. I like things neat. I'll do the kitchen and bathrooms.'

'I'll vacuum then.' Gemma let out a relieved breath. She could use a vacuum cleaner thanks to a kindly au pair once letting her help.

While they dealt with the inside of the house, Sam focused on something outside the back door. Registering her grim expression as she scrubbed, Gemma dragged the cleaner closer, curious to see what she was doing. Catching a chemical stench she flinched, remembering when she'd smelled that stuff last. Why was Sam using it out here? Could it be –? Keep vacuuming, she told herself. Don't think about it, distract yourself. Narrowing her eyes, she scanned the room. Spies posed as cleaners, so what sort of set would this room make for a play?

Once lines of washing were blowing in the wind, floors cleaned and surfaces tidied, over morning coffee Sam brought up the subject of fire.

'I look for it in people,' she said, clipping her words. 'Fire flares up in someone who finds what they love. It keeps them going, lights up the dark times, warms them when the world turns cold. It burns up obstacles too – although it needs good fuel. And fire will scorch if it gets out of hand.' She stared into the distance, then put down her mug and abruptly headed for the beach.

Gemma watched her. She'd never heard her speak that way.

'Maybe fire means a barbecue later?' Alice joked as she and Gemma fixed sandwiches for lunch. Sam still hadn't come back. 'Fire walking? Dancing round a fire?'

Gemma winced. How much did Sam know? They shared a silent meal and cleared up together. Then without explanation, Sam re-appeared and hustled them into the Range Rover, driving at speed across the valley. After a lengthy and mostly silent trip, they stopped outside an art gallery with a large draped banner announcing the exhibition's name – 'Dissent.'

'Today's trip,' Sam spoke at last. She pulled out her wallet and bought three tickets.

Thick, black curtains framed the entrance and sombre music accompanied them into a large display space. After the sunlight outside, it took Gemma several moments to adjust to the dim interior. Skillfully lit photographs confronted them, some almost as big as a door. All were images of protests, rallies, demonstrations and marches, with captions telling their stories. Recorded commentaries or extracts from media reports played alongside the more notable events.

Gemma saw hundreds of medical staff lying prone outside a company's headquarters, staging a 'die-in' over genetic modification. In others, young people had chained themselves to trees about to be illegally logged. The photographer had captured the stark terror in their eyes as hooded figures approached with chainsaws raised. Scores of law students linked arms to blockade a Supreme Court, incensed at a judge's racist verdict and probably aware that their universities would soon expel them. In one picture, a dark-haired girl defied a courtroom full of uniformed Nazis.

'Sophie Scholl, indicted and killed by the National

Socialists for distributing anti-war leaflets –' Alice read aloud.

Gemma shivered and moved ahead on her own. Turning a corner, she came face-to-face with young people being dragged into police vans. Car doors slammed as she heard pounding feet, angry voices, yells of alarm. The smell of fire pricked her nostrils. At a muffled scream she stumbled back, thrusting out her arms, pushing everything away –

'Gemma?' Sam's arm was around her, Alice supporting her from the other side.

Opening her eyes, Gemma stared about. Their part of the gallery was empty apart from themselves. An approaching custodian stopped at a gesture from Sam and continued his patrol. The huge photograph in front of her was a photograph again, silent and still, the recorded commentary over.

'Do you need to go out?' Sam offered.' Get some air?'

Gemma shook her head. 'I thought I saw someone I knew,' she mumbled. 'But I was wrong, it's okay.' Salty tears stung her cheeks. Tears of relief? Or rage? She braced herself, determined to see the rest of the show.

After that, the tone of the photographs changed. In the next section, governments reformed their racist and sexist policies, developers backed away from destructive projects. Manufacturers changed to environmentally friendly products and more humane rulers replaced brutal regimes. An unmistakable message that dissent is effective.

But is it? And what of the protesters? Gemma knew about those moments of triumph, the heady feeling of being heard. But she also knew that issues weren't the only reason that activists did what they did.

'Those people had fire in their bellies,' Sam observed as they left but Gemma left Alice to answer. The shock of that image still churned in her own body, a reaction so violent she couldn't hide it.

Sam's earlier words about fire haunted Gemma during her swim, and as she helped prepare their meal. After they'd eaten and cleared up, she slipped outside to follow the narrowing strip of sand along the beach. The tide was coming in. She'd walk as far as she could, guided by moonlight and the white foam edging the shore. She needed to be on her own. That bloody photo, it had tripped her up. Ripped her open to the real reason she was here.

Out of sight of the house, no longer aware even of the beach, Gemma stood still, seeing once more the running figures outlined by the burning house, feeling the heat of the fire in the cold black night, recoiling at the shouts and sirens. She'd wanted to be bad – but not like this.

Oh, Jacob. He'd lied to her. They'd all lied to her. Falling to her knees, she pounded her fists into the sand. How could they? Would she have made that phone call if she'd known what they planned? Brought the police, caused his arrest?

She collapsed weeping onto the tussocky dunes, replaying the events of that awful night. Confessing to the police why she was there, admitting her association with Jacob. Learning of his deliberate setting of the fire, his willingness to kill.

After that, her parents' appalled intervention and the special measures put in place to keep her, a key witness and a juvenile, invisible during the court hearings so she didn't have to see him. But from behind the screen, she could still hear his voice, that beautiful, dangerous voice.

Jane and Henry did well, got her name suppression, insisted the hours of questioning be recorded so she didn't have to speak in public, even arranged shielding screens in the bleak courtroom. They did everything in their power to protect their daughter, so shamefully allied to the arsonist. Hoped against hope that she was oblivious to his plans, until that evening when she furtively followed him and unsuspectingly made that phone call to the emergency services

Was she oblivious? Deep down, had she suspected what Jacob was capable of? During the trial, Gemma was spotted once as she left the court by a side door, heard the angry recriminations hurled by people she'd seen as friends – 'You bitch, you put him inside.

We'll get you. You'll pay.'

Alone on the beach now, Gemma let every dark feeling rise up and show its face. No more pretending. Her humiliation that she'd been so blind, her fury at being used, panic, fear, resentment, shame, disgust, she sobbed and screamed it out, let everything be swallowed up in the sound of the waves.

Much later, Gemma sensed the dune plants under her cheek, smelled seaweed and heard the swish of the sea. Sitting up, brushing sand from her face, she felt warmer than she had for a very long time. Leaning against a dune, she let herself remember – *him*.

They'd met at a party at a classmate's home. The parents were at a conference and allowed their teenage offspring to 'invite a few friends over.' All very liberal, and Gemma had gone along.

'This young political guy is coming,' her friend Hayley burbled, 'Jacob. Everyone says he's hot. Clever too, he writes articles.'

Gemma spotted him at once, older than the young people present. Perhaps mid-twenties with hooded dark eyes, high cheekbones, longish black hair and that mountain-man stubble. Later she'd understood how he resented even the few minutes spent shaving, resented time spent on anything but talking about his ideas. He was speaking now to a fascinated group and Gemma got a drink and drifted over to stand at the back and listen.

'But stable government is the best guarantee of freedom,' a budding bureaucrat challenged him.

'When the State is the altar of political freedom, like any altar its purpose is sacrifice. In such a case it's human sacrifice,' came the sardonic reply in a deep, accented voice. 'Even in this land, *especially* in this land.'

At the collective gasp from his audience, he raised his eyebrows and looked around. His gaze met Gemma's and held it for a long moment. Its boldness both shocked and thrilled her.

Then someone stammered out another question and he was speaking again, rapping out information with such passion and humour that his audience relaxed, happy with him again. It was well done.

'It's not what he says,' Gemma observed to her friend, after listening some more. 'Although that's challenging enough. It's how he says it. Like it's the most important thing in the world to him. Something he'd die for. He's sensational.'

'He's gorgeous, you're right,' Hayley sighed. 'A bit scary though.'

Much later, Gemma saw the irony of Jacob demanding from his followers the very same sacrifices as the State he so despised. In those early days, she'd just enjoyed his vitality, his wit and the impact of his clever words. So many words. Among them, the reckless and revolutionary words that delighted her. She'd gone to hear him again and again at clandestine venues around the city.

It wasn't long before he singled her out, praised her commitment. Flattered by his attention, she'd been eager to join in making and distributing his newsletters with their invitations to seductive freedoms.

In those early days, she hadn't registered Jacob's own bitter history of limits and loss. No freedoms flourished around him or anywhere in his life story.

When his admirers shrank to a handful, her disquiet grew but she ignored it. Then one melancholy afternoon, a perverse pity pushed her from their shared worktable into his bed, a minor step for him but for Gemma a terrifying move. He'd acted like he owned her after that.

She remembered the strong, hard body that she came to fear, the clever hands that could be cruel, the appraising eyes.

Of course he'd used her, and her parents' social position to get information about people in power. It was information he could get anywhere in this foolish democracy, he assured her. But he preferred hearing it from her. Once he understood the people in this country, he would help them shake off their shackles. He honoured humanity, would never hurt anyone, he claimed.

Yet he'd hurt her, hadn't he? Cared nothing for

putting her at risk. Who would suspect a girl from such a respectable family? So Gemma carried mysterious packages to his room, packages he thrust to one side as though disinterested in them. She'd never once suspected drugs.

Jacob openly scorned all drug users as burned and pathetic. He never touched them, or alcohol either. That he would deal in drugs to fund his rebellion, set fire to a house to intimidate a rival dealer, it still sickened her. At least no one had been killed.

Wanted for crimes in his own country, officials told her later. Deportation was inevitable after his prison term. He wouldn't bother her again.

Gemma could count on 'protection' until she met the terms set by the Court in collaboration with her parents. Otherwise her part in the whole sorry business was over. She should move on.

Jane and Henry had managed everything like the professionals they were, her exclusion from school 'to recover from a traumatic experience,' the counselling, the lot. But unlike the police, they wouldn't let it go. Was Gemma holding anything back? Anything more the authorities should know about? Were there others involved? Surely there was someone else to blame? They pestered her with questions, on and on.

No, no and no, she answered them, I've nothing more to tell you. Why couldn't they accept that *she'd* fallen for his idealism? *She'd* been flattered by his attention and so willingly seduced. Their expensively educated daughter, *she* was the problem, not Jacob. She'd gone into it, eyes wide open. And been horribly wrong.

Self-doubt whispered in her ears at night and she couldn't sleep. Had she suspected Jacob's craziness all along? Played at being an anarchist to get back at her snobbish parents? Just another bored, rich kid, shallow and superficial? Someone might have died in the fire. Perhaps people had already died from Jacob's drugs, with her an accomplice.

More and more, she dreaded the nights with their time to think. Her stomach refused food as her misery grew. And her parents who couldn't even talk openly to her assured her every day that they understood. They understood nothing.

But they had set up this time with Sam. Gemma dug her toes deep into the sand, remembering how she'd fought against their plan.

In this peaceful place, she'd been able to swim to exhaustion and finally sleep. She could even face food again and manage Sam's strange outings. Then the miracle of that theatre visit. For a few hours afterwards, she'd blazed with hope, dreamed of new beginnings. But the photo brought reality crashing back. She wasn't going anywhere except back to her prison at home. And after that?

Gemma sighed. It must be late. She got up to splash her face in a small stream pooling at the base of a cliff.

Then she hesitated. Was she seeing things? Was the water going backwards? No, the moonlight wasn't deceiving her; the incoming tide was pushing against the outgoing trickle. The moon versus gravity, Alice would say.

Gemma swallowed a cupped handful from the water nearest the cliff. Still sweet, the salt hadn't reached it yet. Soon the tide would turn and the stream flow freely into the sea again. As a city girl, she rarely noticed these cycles of tides and seasons or registered their awesome power.

It came to her then, and she knew it to be true. 'I'm part of these great cycles too. I'm *not* stuck.' She heard it as clearly as though the words had been spoken. 'I am changing and moving, even if it doesn't feel like it.'

Splashing her face again with water that now tasted slightly salty, Gemma set off along the shore. Summer wasn't over, anything could happen. And there was still this game that Alice kept grumbling about. Gemma laughed aloud as a name came to her for Alice's gloomy obsession. She'd call it Sam's-Game-whatever-it-is.

She arrived back at the house to find the others in a sombre mood. 'Some idiot left a dead seagull at the back door,' Alice whispered to her. 'With a note tied round its neck, addressed to Sam. Did you see anyone on the beach?'

Gemma shook her head.

'We found it half an hour ago,' Sam added. 'It might have been there all evening.'

'Do you know who left it?' Gemma ventured to Sam. 'Why would anyone do something so sick?'

'Oh yes,' Sam said. 'I know who left it and why. It's a warning to me. I'm to stop helping girls to fly. But we've buried it and I'm off to bed.'

Gemma was only too ready to do the same and avoid any further talk. She sped to the bathroom. Bed and sleep were what she craved. She'd learn more in the morning.

8

ALICE

The next morning over breakfast, no one mentioned the dead seagull. Alice couldn't banish from her mind the image of those blank staring eyes, the huge wings folded close to the lifeless body and the note tied like a luggage label around the bird's outstretched neck. Or Sam's taut expression as she searched the grounds, before stuffing the paper into her pocket.

'It's quite safe, there's no one around,' she'd said. 'Let's bury the poor creature.' She dug a deep hole behind the vegetable garden and buried the bird while Alice held the torch, saying nothing.

Positioning several large stones on top, Sam explained, 'I don't want anything digging it up,' before adding, 'I'm sorry you had to see that, Alice. Someone's sending me a message, but it's nothing for you to worry about.'

'It's horrible. They must hate you.' Alice burst out.

Sam back pushed her hair. 'It's horrible,' she agreed. 'And yes, they probably do.'

Before Alice could ask any more, Gemma arrived from her walk on the beach, face blotchy, eyes swollen and red. More drama, although Gemma looked calm – until she'd been told about the bird. Then she'd raced for the bathroom. It hadn't kept her from sleeping though, while Alice tossed and turned half the night.

Now here was Sam looking fresh and rested as though she hadn't a worry in the world, asking Alice to help her concoct a Cajun recipe after breakfast.

They'd celebrate day seven with an expedition in the boat, Sam said. With a fine day forecast, they could eat their evening meal on the beach when they got back. They might even light a fire for their outdoor picnic, as there were no fire restrictions in place.

So once again Alice was cooking, a one-pot meal of spicy beans, tomatoes and other vegetables. As she chopped and stirred she kept glancing at Gemma, hunched on a chair outside and pretending to read. Alice hadn't seen her turn a page in fifteen minutes. She hadn't said anything about her walk last night but when she woke up, had raved on about Sam's-Game-whatever-it-is, her new name for Sam's mysterious plans for them.

She'd insisted on arranging the outdoor fire too, collected driftwood, set up a tripod with hooks to hold a cooking pot and gone about it with a disturbing single-mindedness. Something was up. The Dissent exhibition had certainly upset her. Had it reminded her of those anarchists?

Alice remembered how she'd glossed over the 'trouble' they'd got into, but there had been an arrest. Also Gemma's parents wouldn't agree easily to her exclusion from school. Alice hadn't wanted to ask more in case she was expected to talk about her own troubles in return.

'Do you know anything about anarchists?' she asked Sam now, as she peeled onions.

'A bit. Why do you ask?'

'Just curious. What are they on about? Do they all wear black?'

'I don't think so. They live by their own ideals with no rules. Very high-minded originally but idealists can attract oddballs. Anarchy's no exception, it's often used as an excuse to just attack society these days. Does that make sense?'

'A bit.'

'You keep looking at Gemma. You're worried about her?' Sam stopped her stirring and studied the distant figure.

Careful, Alice warned herself and held up a knobbly root of ginger. 'No, I just wondered what she's reading. How much shall I grate?'

After lunch they boarded Apsara and cruised up and down the coastline, passing grassy headlands, tall cliffs and hidden sandy bays accessible only by sea. Occasional swimmers dived from moored boats and picnickers sprawled on the sand in isolated inlets. Several people greeted Sam and even Apsara, acknowledging the vessel by name.

They passed boats large and small, some with fishing enthusiasts hunched over rods, intent on their lines. A small group of kayakers skimmed by and Sam chuckled as Alice gazed after them. ' It's easy going with the tide, but I don't envy them the haul back,' she said. 'At least in the tandem canoes, there are two people to paddle.'

Sam held the tiller lightly, alert yet relaxed but she studied each vessel as though looking for someone, and examined the passing coastline. Had last night's unwelcome gift come by sea?

They stopped only once, dropped the anchor and slipped overboard to swim ashore to a perfect half moon of white sand surrounded by rocks. No one else was in sight.

After exploring the beach, Sam and Alice stretched out in the sun. Alice was just drifting off to sleep when Gemma flopped down on the sand beside Sam. 'So who's been spraying graffiti at your house? Is it the same people who left the dead seagull?'

Sam sat up, eyes wide. 'How did you – you couldn't have seen it. I locked the back door.'

'I didn't see it. I smelled the oven cleaner you were using on it. I only know one reason to use oven cleaner outside,' Gemma grimaced. 'And that's to scrub off graffiti. Why didn't you tell us?'

Alice looked from one to the other. What was she missing?

'I didn't want to bother you. It's gone now, and the housework was needed,' Sam countered. 'But yes, it's the same people, I'm almost certain. And now it's over. The note made that clear. They've made their point and that's the end of it. But I've got people keeping an eye on the house for a while, when we're out like this.'

She shook her head and eyed Gemma. 'Anything else? You look like there's more.'

'You didn't seem too happy when Aishe gave you that page at the gypsy fair,' Gemma added. 'And Mikael was worried about you that day on the island.'

Sam exhaled. 'You don't miss much. You'll be a formidable playwright one day, Gemma. All right, I have had some unpleasant incidents lately. Not enough to cancel your time here though.' She glanced at them both. 'I'm fortunate to have people who look out for me, Aishe's family for a start. They're a large clan and one of them heard people asking questions about my work. Aishe gave me their report. And Mikael? He takes an interest in my work too.' She got up. 'Enough for you, Gemma? Let's go back then.'

Alice had obviously underrated her cousin. And what was this work of Sam's? Something to do with flying? She plunged into the sea behind her, anxious to reach the boat and return to the house.

When they clambered onto the jetty half an hour later, two women strolled by, binoculars in hand. 'All clear,' they murmured to Sam as they focused their glasses on some diving seabirds. 'There's been no one near the house all afternoon.'

Sam thanked them and they ambled off. 'Friends,' she explained, securing Apsara's moorings. 'Now for a cup of tea.'

Alice stepped cautiously into the house. Using reopening the windows as an excuse, she checked every room before joining Sam in the kitchen to check on their meal. Would Sam say any more? How could she find out about her work? And why hadn't Gemma said anything about her suspicions?

With the tide full, they all swam in the shallows, warm from the day's sun. Alice got out first to add more wood to Gemma's fire and stir the spicy dish.

Sam and Gemma soon joined her and wrapped in towels, they spooned their food into bowls. Delicious, another recipe for her notebook. Alice would write it down later.

Her meal finished, she rolled over on her towel to let the fire warm her back. The scent of spices mingled with smoke and sea smells, and roosting birds screeched nearby. As perfect an evening as you could imagine.

Gemma gazed out to sea as she ate her second bowl of food. Sam swirled the wine in her glass and stared into the fire as though searching for something. Alice sensed the change in her mood and shivered. Their first seven days were over, so what would happen now?

Sure enough, Sam leaned up on her elbow, her expression unreadable. 'Day Seven, the end of our first week together,' she said.

Gemma put down her bowl and turned around.

'It's been a lively few days,' Sam added. 'I feel you're ready to move on, both of you.'

'Move on where? Leave here?' Alice's throat tightened.

'I hope not. No Alice, move on from the outings. Take the first step in what some women call the Game. If you're willing.'

'So there *is* a game,' Alice breathed.

'You've heard of it?' Sam glanced at her.

'Aishe said something,' she mumbled.

'So she did.' Sam dug in the sand with a stick. 'When women lose their natural place in the world, certain people pass it on to girls who are ready. I'm one of those women and that's why you're here.'

Alice sensed Gemma alert and silent beside her and felt more spooked than she'd expected.

'If you'd grown up in a different community, you'd have absorbed certain qualities naturally,' Sam went on. 'What I'm offering you would have been no big deal, a normal part of a young girl's life. But living as people do now, hidden away in their separate houses, it's not possible.'

'What's not possible? What do we have to –' The pounding fear in her chest had Alice on her feet but Sam interrupted.

'Relax, Alice,' she spoke lightly. 'Learning from a whole community of women isn't possible, that's all. Think of this Game as a gift, no strings attached, something for you to enjoy. Meet me in the front room after we've cleared up.'

After she'd showered and changed into dry clothes, Alice packed away rugs and cushions and put out the fire while the others dealt with the dishes. Then following Gemma into the front room, she joined Sam at the large round table, feeling slightly sick.

'There's lots I could say about the Game but look through these pages first.' Sam tipped out the contents of a large box. 'Take your time and find one person that you like the look of, someone who interests you. When you've chosen, I'll explain a bit more.'

Alice stared at the slippery heap of laminated pages. Each single-sided sheet had a photo with what appeared to be a brief biography above it. All were of women, some young, some old, some in old-fashioned clothes. 'What's this about?'

'Go ahead,' Sam urged. 'Choose someone who appeals to you.'

Alice exhaled irritably and glanced through a dozen or so pages before selecting an older woman with a lively expression. As Alice read about this Lise Meitner being denied the Nobel Prize for being female, her indignation grew. This wasn't centuries ago but in 1944. Lise gained a Doctorate in physics and worked as a nuclear physicist at an Austrian university but wasn't paid because of her gender.

Alice stopped reading for a moment, picturing this woman's life and then finished the page. In letters to her scientist nephew, Lise set out her theory of splitting an atom into its smaller parts, the first person to do so. When a colleague later won the Nobel Prize for originating the theory instead, her name wasn't even mentioned. Only when the old committee records were opened in the 1990's was her exclusion exposed.

Alice sat back and studied the cheerful, open face. Sam leaned over her shoulder to look. 'That photo was taken during a lecture tour, I think,' she said. 'Lise regretted the weapons that came from her research but never her devotion to physics, in spite of the rough deal she got. All those posthumous honours they gave her in 1997 – what would she make of them?'

'What kept her going?' Alice asked. Sam just raised an eyebrow and turned to see Gemma's choice.

9

GEMMA

Gemma skimmed several pages before selecting a striking young blonde gazing resolutely into the camera. Emily Hobhouse, she read, an activist who provoked the British government by exposing conditions in more than one hundred British-run concentration camps. No, that must be wrong. Concentration camps were German, weren't they? From the Second World War? Gemma re-read the paragraph.

But Emily's campaigning began in 1900 and was indeed against concentration camps run by the British fighting Dutch Boers in South Africa. Almost thirty thousand Boer women and children starved to death in these camps, along with countless black Africans.

After campaigning for years, Emily got enough public support from the British people to get some camps closed and the remaining women and children released.

More than a pretty face then. How did she get through to the British people in wartime, with all the patriotic bullshit going on? Gemma read on, a note at the end of the page catching her attention.

In 1921, a gift of money in small coins from Afrikaner women and children helped Emily live out her last few years in a home of her own. Gemma imagined this lovely woman, worn out and weary, getting such a gift. What a play it would make. Her fingers traced the firm chin on the photograph.

'You're thinking about Emily?' Sam's voice brought her back.

'About that gift of money at the end,' Gemma swallowed.

'Yes. They still honour her in South Africa.'

'Yet she wasn't British or even South African,' Gemma insisted. 'A woman of the world, really 'of the world.' '

'Not what those words usually mean?'

'Nations are made-up, they're not even real.'

Sam studied her but made no comment. 'Now that you've both chosen someone I'd like you to find out more about them, if you're willing,' she said instead, touching the pile of pages. 'You can use the library in my office and the two computers there as well. You thought there's no network coverage here but it's 24/7 – when I turn it on.'

Gemma scowled. What a mean trick.

'Why should we?' Alice sat straighter in her chair, chin thrust out. 'I mean, what's it got to do with a game? I don't get this.'

'Several things,' Sam said. 'The first is we'll all share

what you find about these women. Later I'm expecting you'll choose others from this collection. Sharing their stories means we can learn about twice as many.'

'But what's it got to do with a game?' Alice asked again.

'It's the first step.'

'Is that all you're going to tell us?' Alice persisted.

'For now, yes.'

'Both of these women are dead,' Alice kept up her resistance.

'Humour me then, let them live on in your appreciation.' Sam grinned at them both. 'This first part of the Game depends on how you want to play it. This is what I'd like to happen. First you research your choice and then tomorrow evening, show us something about how your woman survived and thrived, in spite of all the obstacles in her life. And there'll be plenty of those.'

'What do you mean by *show*?' Alice, still suspicious.

'I'm coming to that. In my office along with books and computers, you'll find a large wardrobe full of costumes, clothing, accessories, even a wig or two.' Sam's eyes sparkled with mischief.

'Dress-up clothes? You're kidding?' Gemma bolted upright, eyes wide.

'If you like, or you could call them props to help your lessons come alive. Feel free to become your character or an observer of her life, or even a commentator of her time, but really get into how she got through her challenges. Then surprise us.' Her tone changed. 'We're in for some rough weather by the way, there's been a severe storm warning. We might even get cut off for a day or two, so this is one way to spend the time.'

'A storm? I hate storms.' Alice hurried to the window to study the sky, black with scudding clouds.

Gemma's thoughts were still with Emily Hobhouse. With props, she'd be able to flesh out the scenes forming in her mind. 'You mentioned computers?' she reminded Sam.

'Yes, one each, and they're both connected to the printer. I've left the password on the keyboard. Obviously you've a week's missed messages to catch up on, but would you limit your social media time for now, until your research is done? We'll talk some more in the morning.'

So Sam's-Game-whatever-it-is had begun? Gemma couldn't see anything sinister in it. A strange task, but she might as well learn about Emily Hobhouse if they were going to be stuck indoors.

10

ALICE

In bed that night, Alice closed the curtains against the storm and made notes in her journal, glad she'd chosen Lise Meitner from among the pages. She'd enjoy researching an intelligent woman, now they had computer access. An inauspicious introduction to Sam's-Game-whatever-it-is, but Alice could be patient. If Sam did turn out to be a shrink, she'd still thwart her somehow. After that awful time when her mother so willingly hung the 'depressive' label on her, Alice knew all about offhand diagnosis. Not once had those doctors taken time to understand what really tipped her into the dark.

She glanced at her cousin, lying against her pillows and staring into her notebook. 'What did you make of tonight?' she asked, keeping her tone light. 'All those women? See, I was right, there is a game.'

Not looking up, Gemma replied absently, 'Yeah, a bit different from what I expected. Good news about the computers though. We can get our mail, even though we can't use our phones.'

Alice's tapped her pen on her notebook, doubting

she'd have many messages. 'What about the game then?'

'Doesn't make any sense to me,' Gemma said. 'You?'

'Nope,' Alice agreed. 'I still can't figure out what she's up to. One week down and lots to go.'

'It's been one of the best weeks of my life,' Gemma offered a rare smile. 'Sam's so laidback. It's great being with an adult who doesn't get wound up just by looking at me, like I'm a bomb about to go off or something.'

Alice raised an eyebrow. 'Don't you try to scare people? Isn't that what all the black's about, and the moods?'

Gemma actually laughed and Alice, encouraged, added, 'But I know what you mean about Sam. She doesn't study what I eat, I don't think she even cares. Tracey comments on every mouthful like it's radioactive.'

Gemma opened her mouth to speak, then hesitated.

'Go on, say it,' Alice encouraged.

'You – you don't seem to eat much,' Gemma ventured. 'At the Food Fair or anywhere. You don't snack either, I mean, we're sharing a room.'

'And you'd know if I had chocolate stashed away? Well, I haven't. I've had my reasons for getting this big.'

'You're not –?' Gemma stared at her, eyes wide.

'Pregnant?' Alice guessed. 'No, I'm not.' Her throat closed up and she couldn't go on.

'Your business, sorry.'

Alice blew her nose and shook her head, trying to clear it. She needed to talk. 'What about the woman you chose, Emily?'

'Mmm,' Gemma turned her notebook around so that Alice could see.

The pages were crammed with meticulous sketches showing a tiny Emily Hobhouse moving through different frames, snippets of conversation rising in speech bubbles above her head.

'So that's what you do all the time? They're good,' Alice bent closer to look. 'I didn't know you could draw like this. These are like storyboards.'

'What's a storyboard?'

Did she really not know? 'Scenes for a film.'

'I just draw cartoons, always have.'

'What about?'

'Just stuff I think about,' Gemma sounded vague.

'People? What they do?'

'Yeah, I draw people.'

'Take a look at this then. Imagine looking so cheerful after one of your colleagues walks off with your Nobel Prize?' Alice flourished the page about Lise Meitner, not hiding her indignation.

Gemma put down her pencil and studied the photo.

'So how would you draw her? ' Alice asked.

'I haven't read her story,' Gemma said, passing it back. 'I'd draw her with her chin up, I guess. A bit like this photo.'

Alice put the page on the bedside table. 'I'd never speak to those colleagues again. What do you make of the dressing up, then?'

'Sam's full of surprises,' Gemma yawned. 'No dressing up with my parents, that's probably why I wear all this.' She gestured at her discarded black clothes. 'If dressing up is part of this game you're so obsessed with, it's harmless enough. It could be fun.'

Alice hated the idea. She glanced down at her legs. 'Nothing will fit me.'

'Wait and see,' Gemma's voice sounded almost kind as she put her notebook down and turned out her bedside light.

Alice lay awake for a long time, going over the past week, the outings and now this odd game. So far Sam had been firm but not bossy, relaxed about situations that would have thrown her own mother into hysterics. The graffiti, the seagull and this storm warning, for a start. She didn't comment on Gemma's ups and downs or her own hostile questions. Alice had no sense of being criticised or judged. So why did the idea of Sam's-Game-whatever-it-is freak her out?

She peered out between a gap in the curtains at the black, racing clouds and elusive sickle moon, shivering at the wild beauty of the sky. If only she hadn't overheard those words from her mother.

11

GEMMA

'How long do we have to talk about these women?' Gemma asked next morning over the noise of the storm. Almost impossible to concentrate as summer lightning flashed, thunder rumbled overhead and heavy rain pelted against the windows.

'Take as long as you need,' Sam said. 'Entertain us as much as you want. We're already marooned, it's not unusual. One stretch of road goes under water and then the bridge gets flooded as well until the tide turns. Even when the water's gone, the bridge has to be checked before we can drive over it. We can't take the boat out in a storm either.'

She spread her arms. 'Nothing to worry about though. The house doesn't leak and we won't starve. I even have an emergency generator if the electricity goes off. Why don't you both research your women now? The Internet's working, I checked earlier. I've got another project on so I won't need the office at all. You've got the whole day.'

She pulled something from her pocket and shuffled her hands together. 'I've a shell in one hand, whoever chooses the correct one will go first tonight.'

Gemma chose the wrong hand. 'Great, I'll need all the time I can get.' She aimed for a casual tone. 'I haven't seen the props yet, but can we borrow other things for our show?'

'What kind of things?'

'Oh, a sheet or a blanket or two?'

'There's plenty in the linen cupboard.' Sam poured herself more coffee and glanced out the window. 'I'll light the fire later if it gets cold.'

Gemma escaped to Sam's office as soon as she could. It turned out to be a spacious room with loads of desk space, overflowing bookshelves and a double wardrobe along one wall with drawers underneath. The props maybe?

She skimmed her messages on Sam's laptop, predictable ravings from friends plus a few lines from her parents. She'd answer them later. Now for Emily Hobhouse and her script.

Alice arrived, sighing with pleasure as she settled at the desktop computer. Then Gemma forgot everything but Emily, until Sam called them down for lunch.

After bolting down a quick sandwich, Gemma hurried back to search through the props. The wardrobe had full-length mirrors inside both doors and she held up various garments in front of herself.

'Come on,' she urged Alice who'd joined her. 'Take a look, there's loads of cool stuff here.'

Alice held back. 'Try these,' Gemma held out two flowing gowns, one in rich green velvet, the other in glistening black with trimmings of jet beads.'

'Aren't you wearing the black?' Alice held the dresses at arm's length.

'Not this time,' Gemma peered at herself in a long drab brown skirt and jacket. She tied a plain apron around her waist.

'You look like van Gogh's Peasant Girl,' Alice observed. 'Want a scarf for your head?' She rummaged in the drawers and found a plain kerchief to cover Gemma's black hair.

Gemma added a straw bonnet and stood back to survey the effect.

'Who're you meant to be?' Alice asked. 'Emily Hobhouse?'

'Wait and see,' Gemma pushed the hat back off her face. Still in the costume, she rummaged amongst the garments, pulling out more items and tossing them into a pile. 'I need these too. You'd better be quick if you want any of this.' She sorted her pile as Alice pulled the black gown over her head and tugged it down past her hips.

Her props complete, Gemma searched on the computer for language clips. Using a headset, she listened and silently mouthed some words. She caught Alice watching her, baffled. 'Are you singing?' her cousin asked.

'Practising my Transvaal accent,' Gemma answered, clicking onto replay for the sixth time.

Alice twirled a 'You're crazy' gesture with a finger as she turned back to the wigs, jewellery, and bags. She'd put the black dress to one side along with an old-fashioned beaded evening bag and shawl and even tried on a few hats before tidying her share of the chaos back into the cupboard.

After their evening meal, Alice disappeared to get ready while Gemma helped Sam clear up. To distract herself, she traded guesses with Sam about how Alice might present the Austrian scientist.

Stately and dignified in the black evening gown, Alice introduced herself as Lise Meitner's friend and an admirer of her devotion to this strange field of study.

'Physics was new to all of us in those days, and I could talk about her theories,' she said, 'But what impressed me is how highly Lise valued it, at huge personal cost to her, some might think. No children, no husband, no status, little recognition, but she didn't miss out.'

Alice explained how Max Planck, known for his quantum theory, chose Lise as his assistant once she'd gained her doctorate. Her remarkable research earned her the nickname of the German Marie Curie, even although she worked unpaid because of her gender.

Telling Lise's story up to and beyond the 1944 Nobel

Prize, Alice added simple explanations and scarcely glanced at her notes. Physics meant zilch to Gemma yet Alice described it readily. How that 'fat equals stupid' situation must have hurt.

'Lise had great regard for her teachers,' Alice concluded. 'She described one professor as so enthusiastic that she discovered a new and wonderful world through him. I'm happy to say she's done the same for me.'

Sam and Gemma applauded wildly and Alice offered an elegant curtsey in return. 'I enjoyed that,' she told them. 'She's a woman worth talking about.'

Gemma suggested they go to the kitchen and give her a few minutes to set up. 'I'll shout when I'm ready.' She never forgot the looks on their faces when ten minutes later, she stepped out from behind the sheets serving as tent walls and as backdrops on her impromptu stage.

Bundles of clothing to replicate women and children in makeshift beds lay about. Gemma, dressed as a Boer woman, gave her introduction to Emily Hobhouse. Using her new Afrikaans accent, she told of the beautiful young English aristocrat who'd given up home, family, wealth and status to help both the Boer and black women and children imprisoned at the command of Lord Kitchener, a British Army officer.

'She saw us dying daily from starvation and disease, almost half a million women, children and men.'

Gemma's eyes stung with real tears. 'She reported everything back to her contacts in the British Parliament and media, insisting that segregation of any race by colour or class must lead to disaster. Few listened.'

She described the hostility from government and the press that greeted Emily on her return to England, and how only pressure from ordinary people helped to get the camps closed and survivors supported.

'There are countless people who would not have been born, but for Emily,' she told her rapt audience. 'Some say she had no children: I say she had thousands.'

Then came the part of the story that moved her most, the gift of small coins from the Afrikaner people that bought a destitute Emily a house in Cornwall, where she lived until her death in 1926. 'There were no mourners at her cremation, no clergymen,' Gemma concluded. 'Only the undertaker who shipped the casket with her ashes back to South Africa. It was installed with honour in front of thousands at the National Women's Monument at Bloemfontein but her death went unreported in the Cornish Press.'

The story over, she stood motionless, her body stooped with sorrow. The moment lengthened. Did they hate it? Gemma held her breath until applause exploded in the room.

'I couldn't move,' Alice cried.

'You had me under a spell,' Sam agreed. 'Gemma, you have a rare gift.'

'You should see the drawings she did for this,' Alice added.

Later, after admiring what Gemma still claimed were just cartoons, Sam praised them again for their efforts. 'It's a lot to ask of you, this first stage of the Game. You got into the spirit of your women, it's a fine start. Ready to choose some more?' She pointed at the table where the box of pages still lay.

12

ALICE

'Do you analyse our choices?' Alice heard the hard edge creep back into her voice as she considered the pages on the table. 'Is that what this game's about?' She adjusted the black gown.

Sam glanced at her as she answered, 'No Alice, I'm not analysing either of you or your choices. I'm inviting you to get to know some of these women.' She waved away Alice's splutter of protest. 'If it helps, imagine them being in your neighbourhood and choose women you'd like to talk to, ask their advice. Find out what kept them going, if you can. They didn't have it easy, any more than you two do.'

Don't act so suspicious, Alice cautioned herself. She'll never let her guard down.

Typical Gemma, oblivious to the atmosphere, sifted through the pile. She'd taken off the scarf but still wore her Boer clothing. 'So many radical women, all new to me,' she murmured.

And you, the anarchist, Alice thought and turned back to Sam. 'How did you find them all?' she asked, keeping her tone pleasant. 'It must have taken ages.'

'They found me, Alice,' Sam said. 'One by one over the years, they made their way into the Game.'

'So what's the plan now?'

'I'd like you to choose a dozen altogether. You won't have to talk about them all. It's not going to rain that long. But choose now, introduce us to a few of them over the next few days like you did tonight. By the end of your time here, we'll all know something new about some remarkable women.'

Alice contented herself with a cynical lift of her eyebrows and returned to sifting through the pages, curious about who she'd select. She wanted to make random choices but something in certain faces or a phrase in the biographies attracted her. Not very scientific and yet there were quite a few scientists in her final choice.

Once they each had their twelve women, Sam joined them again. 'I don't need to look at your choices,' she said. 'But I will tell you this. You've responded to something in these women and that's a key in the Game.'

'We're always responding to something,' Alice objected. 'What's the big deal about that?'

'Attraction's a mysterious thing, Alice. It's worth discovering why people attract us, why we respond to them, why some individuals even inspire us.'

Alice wasn't convinced and saw Gemma's eyes widen in alarm.

'For a start, something mattered more to these women than approval. They defied their families and society for it.' Sam said. 'Oh, they're heroes now, but they weren't in their lifetimes.'

She glanced at them both. 'Everyone needs support to live so courageously, especially girls. Even in our modern culture. Ask yourself, could these women help *you* be the best you can? Perhaps you've instinctively chosen those who would do that?'

Alice didn't answer and Gemma muttered something she couldn't hear.

Sam stretched and got up to go. 'You've chosen your twelve, so learn about them. Make a few notes and we'll talk some more tomorrow. When the weather breaks, we've someone flying in to meet you both, by the way. There's a small airfield on a farm nearby, and a barn where she stores her Piper when she visits. I have shares in it.'

'Shares in the plane or the barn? And is this about the game?' Alice asked, instantly alert.

Sam laughed. 'Shares in the plane, and I even fly it sometimes. And yes Alice, she's part of the Game, also an old friend of mine.'

'Is the plane anything to do with that dead seagull?' Alice asked, earning an appraising glance.

'The warning wasn't about that sort of flying but very perceptive of you, all the same.'

'You said you'd tell us more about your game and

why you do it.' Alice pressed, encouraged. 'We've done what you asked. Can't you tell us now?'

'Explain why I do this? Yes, why not.' Sam sat down again, pushed back her hair and frowned. 'A long time ago, someone helped me, that's why I do it. I was a bit younger than you two.'

Alice rearranged her pages and waited, holding her breath. Surely there'd be more?

'I don't remember my mother, she died when I was very small,' Sam cleared her throat. 'My schoolteacher father didn't re-marry. He took to working in small country schools where we'd have a house provided and a housekeeper to care for me. Not much help for single parents back then. He wasn't a demonstrative man and once I was clean, fed and in school he left me alone. We had very little money and seldom travelled to town. The only women I met were farmers, good, kind, hard-working women but I couldn't see myself as one of them.'

Sam in dungarees? Alice hid a smile.

'I was a wild teenager, lonely, often bored. Very few others to hang out with,' Sam eyed them. 'Just when things were at their worst, my mother's oldest friend rescued me. I didn't know Fran had kept an eye on me from a distance, all those years. She swooped in at the very moment I needed her, invited me to spend time with her in the city. My father was relieved to see me safe with someone else.'

She dropped her gaze and twisted loose strands of her hair. 'He died a few months later, a road accident. I stayed on with Fran and finished my schooling, and we travelled a bit. She also introduced me to a range of superb women, role models I suppose you'd call them.'

Sam smoothed the remaining pages, her expression soft. 'I was angry. Without Fran's help, I'd have harmed myself and others. I owe her a lot.'

Alice gulped. Sam, of all people?

'Why were you angry?' Gemma voiced the question for her.

'Several reasons. Mainly because I'd been taught to obey a system that disadvantages too many people. And I'd been raised for a role that asked very little of me. The best of me wasn't wanted. I didn't like it then and I don't like it now.'

No doubt of that! Alice registered the flash in those blue eyes. 'Those role models, how did they help? Were they real or –?' Alice gestured at her pages.

'Yes, alive and human,' Sam laughed. 'Fran knew all kinds of people. Artists and musicians and also women of science, journalists, businesswomen. I learned from them all. And I learned to value what they stirred up in me.'

'I don't understand,' Alice frowned.

'When we admire someone, something in us wakes up and we grow. But to stay awake, we need spirited people around us to spur us on. Well-behaved, docile, obedient ladies just won't do it.' Sam leaned back in her chair, chuckling.

'About that attraction?' Gemma's voice, so husky Alice could hardly hear her.

'Yes?' Sam turned to her.

'What if it's to bad stuff?'

'Say more?' Sam prompted.

'A while ago I heard this radical guy speaking about injustice, I couldn't get enough of it. That must have been attraction. But he turned out to be bad news, really bad.' Her face took on its hostile mask. 'So what does that make me?' she demanded. 'Being attracted to shit like him? Stupid? And gullible? I did criminal things because of that attraction.'

'Criminal things? Are you sure?' Sam's tone was mild.

'I don't *know*,' Gemma turned on her, eyes fierce. 'I collected packages for him, they might have been drugs. He turned out to be a dealer although he didn't touch them himself.' She swung around to Alice. 'But there was a fire, people could have been killed. I – I was a witness. Now he's in prison for arson and drug dealing.' She gulped. 'So much for attraction. If that's what your game's about, it's crap and I'm the wrong person for it.'

'Oh Gemma,' Sam exhaled. 'That was hard. But tell me, was it him you couldn't get enough of? Or hearing what he had to say about injustice?'

'You liked Emily for standing up against it,' Alice added. Gemma looked awful, about ready to throw up.

'What he said, I suppose,' Gemma muttered after a pause. 'It woke me up. But he didn't match up to his words.' She lifted her chin. 'So I was still an idiot.'

Sam raised an eyebrow. 'Was he charismatic?' she teased. 'Charming and persuasive? Tall, dark and handsome with a foreign accent?'

'How did you know?' Gemma gasped. Alice couldn't follow them. How had Sam known about this?

'You're not the first girl to be schmoozed by a skilfull storyteller,' Sam grinned. 'Or to mistake the storyteller for the story. Think of history's most warped preachers. I've been taken in by one or two charming con men and so have most women I know. It's not a crime, not even your fault. We weren't raised to trust our instincts. But we can learn.'

Gemma's face turned scarlet and Alice saw her fists clench. Surely Sam would ease up on her teasing? But she didn't relent.

'Everyone feels shame at some time, Gemma. Shame means something's been hurt and needs to be mended. But shame's a friend, and anger too, when it's anger for justice. Be glad of it, there's not enough of it around.' She got up. 'Without it, people haven't enough fire to use their gifts. You have, by the way,' she added, heading for the door.

13

GEMMA

Gemma made it to their room without throwing up. She flung her pages on the floor and dived under the bedcovers fully clothed, pulling the sheet over her head. Closing her eyes, she focused on the sound of the sea, letting the churning in her stomach subside. So anger and shame were *good?* News to her. Jane and Henry had made a three act tragic opera out of everything that happened with Jacob.

What of the shame, Gemma? Had you no shame, mixing with people like that? Didn't you care about shaming your parents, shaming your school, our friends, shaming the whole human race?

And she'd had her own shame, different but deep. Shame for being naive, for wanting approval so desperately that she'd been taken in by Jacob. Yet Sam was okay with shame? And anger? Even okay with her, in spite of the drugs and everything?

Alice crept in and undressed. Hearing her getting into bed Gemma pulled down the sheet, meeting Alice's apprehensive gaze.

'I'm fine,' she said. 'More shocked than angry.

Everyone's disapproved of me in one way or another, my parents, the anarchists, the school, but Sam didn't care. Even when I said her game's crap.'

'Sam's-Game-whatever-it-is?' Alice offered a relieved smile. 'Do you really think it's crap?'

'I don't know what it is,' Gemma admitted.

'It was brave, telling us all that. Were you scared?'

'I've been more scared about becoming a shitty human being.' Gemma meant it. She needed to talk. 'Sam's own story, what did you make of it?'

'It's hard to imagine her a poor country kid. Look at her now, with this house, a Range Rover, a boat – and part-shares in a plane.'

'Sounds like she's lucky Fran turned up,' Gemma agreed.

'I didn't know about what you told us,' Alice returned to Gemma's story. 'I won't say anything.'

'Jane and Henry kept everything quiet,' Gemma reminded her. 'And I didn't know about the drugs and the private war Jacob had going with this other guy.'

'So what happened?' Alice ventured. 'If you're okay talking about it.'

'I followed him one night,' Gemma explained about overhearing a meeting being planned and her annoyance at not being invited. Then the excitement of leaving her room late at night, deactivating the house alarms and going out into the dark. Running through the empty streets in her black clothes to the address she'd overheard. The shock of seeing the first flames appear and her instinctive impulse to pull out her phone and call for help.

'I didn't know arsonists stay around to watch their fires so they caught him easily,' she admitted. 'I didn't even know it was arson until later. Whichever way I look at the whole mess, I was a fool.'

'Was he really tall, dark and handsome with a foreign accent?'

'Oh yes,' Gemma groaned. 'All that and more.'

'Then you're not the only idiot on the planet, from what Sam said,' Alice said. 'Nothing shocks her anyway. And Mikael came here one night, and he's tall, dark and handsome with a foreign accent.'

'Did he?' Gemma sat up, all nausea gone. 'I knew there was something going on with those two. How do you know?'

'I heard him talking when I got up for a drink. I'd know that voice anywhere.' She sighed. 'He's no con man.'

'You just love scientists,' Gemma said, feeling better. 'D'you want one of my drawings of him to carry round next to your heart?' She dodged the pillow Alice flung at her. 'Well, it looks like I'm not going to get chucked out, in spite of mixing with criminals. I'm glad you asked Sam about the game, but I still don't get it.'

She got out of bed and retrieved her twelve pages, spreading them on the bed. 'I like Emily and your Lise, so what does that mean? How many more of yours are from Europe?' She counted her own.

'Three,' Alice said, shuffling through her set. 'You?'

'Four, plus two Brits. Do they still count as Europeans?'

Alice shrugged. 'I guess not. I've got one Brit, she's a cosmonaut. And one lawyer, an Iranian.'

'A lawyer? Lucky you,' Gemma sniffed. 'I don't remember seeing her. Mine are a mixed lot.'

'Anything in common? We should look for clues.'

Gemma re-arranged her pages, 'Mostly artists of some sort, writers, musicians. Several are pacifists. I like the look of them all. And you?'

'Scientists, some of them. Quite a few doing work that men usually do, I don't know if that means anything.'

'Why shouldn't you choose scientists, you're practically one yourself? Look at this lovely old Polish woman, she saved Jewish kids from the death camps.' Gemma admired the chubby face.

'Another concentration camp? There's a theme.'

No way. Gemma had just chosen faces she liked, even the pouting British writer who wrote scandalous plays and spied for Charles II. Another playwright? That was more like it. She smiled, remembering Sam and Alice so willing to be captured by her portrayal of Emily and the camps. Wait until they saw what else she planned to show them.

The next day they worked on their research and presentations, meeting up with Sam at meal times. No one mentioned Gemma's revelation, to her relief.

That evening, Alice introduced them to Margaret Hamilton, a young American who developed the current model of computer software engineering at MIT and rose to lead the 400-strong team responsible for software on the Apollo space program. Gemma enjoyed her mimicking of Margaret's playfulness.

'We don't often hear personal things about scientists,' Sam said afterwards. 'Letting her daughter play with the Apollo simulation software and what happened afterwards, that's a great story.'

Gemma also chose a living person, Dolores Huerta, a Mexican-born activist working for poor US farm workers. She portrayed Dolores herself, telling a tale of racism and brutality in 1970's America and conveying her dignified pleasure at winning so many reforms. Listed among the world's 100 greatest women. Dolores survived being attacked, and imprisoned yet continued to celebrate her 'membership in one humanity' and her eleven children.

Sam and Alice praised her performance again, especially her accent. 'I copied a Mexican on Netflix,' Gemma admitted. 'I don't know what Dolores sounds like.' She stirred the hot chocolate Sam had made for them. 'This is the best way to learn about history, getting inside the skins of famous people.'

'Yes, although these women aren't your average celebrities,' Sam reminded her. 'They make it into the Game on their own merits, not because society gave them any stamp of approval. Quite the opposite, usually. Most were tested young, as you're finding out. That's when they build up the emotional strength to thrive, not just survive.'

She glanced at Alice, then Gemma, 'How much has been asked of you, I wonder? Were you threatened as youngsters, except by the usual childhood complaints and a few family dramas? No famine, war or revolution? Me neither. But I still demand the best from myself. That's what I like seeing in everyone.'

The best of us again, Gemma frowned. No one wanted the best of her. Maybe not even herself?

'While the storm's with us, study your women and think about why you chose them,' Sam said. 'I'm still suggesting that like attracts like. Something in you recognised qualities in them. Enjoy finding out. The more you enjoy yourselves, the better company these women will be for you.'

The rain continued for several days, keeping them all indoors. Gemma and Alice used the time to learn about the women they'd chosen.

Gemma's group ranged from a contemporary Japanese feminist to a German mystic. Each woman intrigued her, and choosing which to speak about wasn't easy.

Alice also admitted to being captivated by her British cosmonaut, a Russian mathematician and the woman credited with founding the modern environmental movement.

Ransacking the props cupboard, they changed costumes several times a day and took turns in telling their tales. Sam proved to be an indefatigable listener and generous with her comments but said little more about the Game.

Gemma stopped thinking about it and threw herself into creating her plays. She'd almost forgotten Sam's comment about attraction. Then watching Alice one evening, she glimpsed her cousin with her defences down. Whether she knew it or not, Alice had the very same qualities that she valued in the women she'd chosen. With her delight in the natural world, attentive curiosity, quick wit and easy humour about herself, Alice would fit right in with them if they met. Did she know?

Gemma considered her own women. A creative articulate bunch, they refused to be silenced, risked scorn, even danger, to expose injustice. Was the same impulse in her? The idea warmed a cold place deep inside her. Yet feeling good about herself also felt strange, almost wrong. Enjoying writing her scripts so much seemed a bit selfish too. But she'd follow this instinct for theatre, or be miserable all her life.

In spite of everything they'd shared, Alice still couldn't unwind around Sam. After their shows Gemma listened and sketched while the two of them argued, although Alice called it discussion.

'Has anything changed for women, with feminism?' Alice demanded one evening. 'Margaret Hamilton and Dolores Huerta lived through feminism in the US and they're still fighting for a fair deal.'

'Change takes time,' Sam agreed.

'What's changed since Lise Meitner's day?' Alice persisted.

Did Alice ask these questions just to show off? Gemma couldn't keep up with her and Sam said nothing.

'Why are you doing this?' Alice tried another approach, still seeking a reaction. 'Spending time and money taking us to places, and now getting us to learn about these women?'

'I explained earlier that when I needed more role models, someone helped me,' Sam answered.

'I guess so. But why choose us?' Alice persisted.

'Because I was asked to, and when I made some enquiries you both interested me.'

'Who asked you?' Alice wouldn't be put off.

Sam put down her wine glass and straightened in her chair. 'Gemma's parents asked me, Alice. Jane and Henry met me years ago when they stayed here with a mutual friend, Gemma came too. Since then they've learned from other lawyers about my work with young women. They employed me.'

'They *paid* you?' Gemma exploded, finding her voice at last. 'Alice is right, this *is* a summer camp for bad girls. You're just another do-gooder therapist, you don't even want us here.' Her hands trembled so much her notebook fell to the floor.

'As it happens, I'm very choosy about who I spend time with. I don't offer my home to everyone. I'm enjoying your company, and I'm not a therapist,' Sam said.

Gemma glared at her. What a fool she'd been, suckered again.

'But you've been paid to fix us, admit it.' Alice snapped,

'You don't need fixing,' Sam gazed back, unruffled by their fury. 'But there have been some gaps in your lives I'm helping to fill, after that it's up to you. I'm not forcing you to do anything, not even to stay.'

'Do you report on us?' Alice's voice had a mutinous tone. 'We're allowed to see any reports if you do.'

'You're here on trust,' Sam said. 'Your parents trust me, I trust them not to interfere and I trust you to use this time and begin to trust yourselves. That's a whole lot of trust. And there are no written reports.'

'No one trusts us,' Gemma said, her stomach churning. 'Jane and Henry would have me computer-chipped if they could.'

'Gemma, they're lawyers in an industry based around reasonable doubt, they don't 'do' trust,' Sam's voice remained calm.

'What about verbal reports then?' Alice persisted, pushing back her chair and getting up from the table.

'What about being your own report?' Sam fired at her, eyes blazing. 'What about dropping this fixation about what other people think and understand yourself, warts and all?'

'I don't have warts –' Alice protested then grabbed a cushion and hugged it, giggling until Gemma feared she might choke. 'I'm having the best summer of my life and I'm arguing about it?' she gasped, flopping down on the couch. 'I'm crazy.'

Sam's expression softened and she stretched and yawned. 'You'll make a fine scientist,' she said to Alice, then turned to Gemma. 'I can see that you're shocked about this, Gemma, but please stay. It's dangerous out there in this weather. And nothing has changed. I meant it when I said I'm enjoying your company, however you came to be here.'

How did she guess I might make a run for it? Gemma kept her face impassive.

'We can speak more about this but later, please.' Sam yawned again. 'I need to go to bed, I stayed up too late last night.'

When she'd gone, Gemma turned to Alice. 'You were right, I'm sorry,' she admitted. 'Our parents were up to something all along. I missed all the signs, too busy fighting with mine. I didn't imagine this, Sam being paid to have us here. All for money, it's so typical.'

Alice shook her head, still clutching her cushion. 'We knew our families would cover our costs this summer. Sam has to live. I still want to find out what this game's about, so I don't care.' She threw the cushion at Gemma. 'I hope you'll stay.'

Gemma caught it and hugged it to her. The wind had dropped, the driving rain turned to squally showers. She'd stopped counting the seconds between lightning and the cracks of thunder. Would she?

14

ALICE

The morning light revealed a riot of fluffy clouds, calm seas and sunshine – and Gemma asleep in her bed, her usual chaos of clothes around her. No signs of late night packing. Relieved, Alice dressed quietly. Still early.

She picked up her twelve pages from the bedside table. As Sam said, nothing had changed. So what if Jane and Henry had paid for them to have a summer at the beach learning about Sam's-Game-whatever-it-is. She'd nothing to lose, she'd take Sam's advice and have fun with it.

Alice liked her women, but twelve were a lot to remember and their lives spread over centuries as well as countries. She decided to make them members of an exclusive women's club. Picturing them meeting, she imagined the details they'd share. What did it matter, the years and geography that separated them? They'd appreciate each other. She managed an hour at the computer before breakfast, getting her notes in order.

'My friend's flying in later today,' Sam reminded them over toast and tea. 'Do you feel up to some company and trying something new? Taking a break from your women? She trains girls in useful skills, I think you'll enjoy it.'

'It's part of this game, I suppose? We call it Sam's-Game-whatever-it-is, Gemma's idea,' Alice said. 'I'll give it a go.'

Gemma concentrated on her food and didn't look up.

Sam lingered at the table. 'I'm glad you're both staying,' she admitted. I've enjoyed seeing how you view your women, I've learned a lot about them.'

'And about us?' Alice couldn't resist the dig.

'I'm more interested in you learning that about yourselves,' Sam grinned back. 'From where I'm sitting, you're both fine.'

'You've done this before, so what's one thing shared by all the women in your box?' Alice asked.

Sam threw up her hands in mock defence. 'All of them? You've nothing easier to ask me at this early hour?' She paused for a moment. 'Social pressure, then. Some social pressures never change, no matter when or where we appear. How women look is one. Men have defined the ideal female body for centuries, and women almost always fall for it. Even though that ideal keeps changing.'

'And isn't based on real women?' Gemma interposed. So she had been listening.

Sam nodded. 'You're right, and of course there's an ideal for men too. Artists can say they're creating archetypes out of their dreams, but women still take that image as a goal.'

'And fall short?' Gemma added.

Sam nodded. 'When they're judged by their bodies, women suffer most. Another pressure is a so-called ideal female behaviour, men usually decide that too. It gets altered to suit the situation. Think of wartime.'

'Women do men's work while they're at war, then get thrown back in the kitchen when it's over.' Gemma's voice rose to a feverish pitch.

'Something like that,' Sam rested her chin in her hand. 'Most women either conform to these ideals or fight them, but I rarely see anyone question who sets the standards and why. Or ask why, by the time their daughters grow up, the ideal's changed. It's not surprising mothers and daughters frustrate each other.'

Her gaze rested on Gemma again. 'Your mother fought to be a lawyer and keep working after you were born, Gemma. Lots of people saw her as a rebel.'

Gemma grimaced. 'You're kidding. Jane loves all the stuffy lawyer rules. I'd say she's a total conformist, and she's planning a mother and daughter partnership so I can be the same.'

Scowling, she leaned back and crossed her arms. Alice didn't envy her trying to persuade her bossy mother into changing any plans.

'And you, Alice?' Sam asked.

Alice shifted in her chair, her throat dry. She couldn't speak.

'You've a grasp of science many people would envy,' Sam said. 'And the skill to explain it. I learned more about physics listening to you than I would have believed possible. You sound as though you genuinely love science.' She raised a quizzical eyebrow.

'It helps me relax,' Alice admitted, pleased by her praise. 'Feeling that I belong in nature.'

'And your mother?' Sam murmured. 'Does Tracey know this?'

Alice shook her head. 'She lives for my brothers.'

'But your teachers? They enjoy your interest?'

'A few,' Alice admitted. 'I get good grades, one or two let me loose in the labs.'

'That's good to hear,' Sam got up. 'I'll go up to the farm now, I'm expecting the plane very soon.'

Sam's visitor turned out to be a young woman called Denise who introduced herself as a self-defence instructor.

'Self-defence skills are vital to the Game' Sam explained. 'They might save your life one day. Have you had any training before? No? Then Denise can teach you the basics, she's staying with us for a few days. You can trust her.'

Alice and Gemma exchanged glances. Weird and weirder, Gemma's expression said but Alice trembled as excitement bubbled up. This was new.

Denise pushed back the furniture in the front room

with an ease that suggested she'd done it before. 'We'll start with stereotypes about women.' She smiled at them. 'I guess you're already talking about those with Samantha?'

Alice nodded, she liked this cheerful woman already. Gemma just stared.

'Assaults on women are common, because of the assumption that women are more passive and won't fight back,' Denise tossed her head. 'Stereotype Number One. Both men and women have that one. But self-defence is more than just okay, it's an intelligent, ethical decision.'

She explained the background to her methods. Then using Sam as her partner, she demonstrated routines that left Alice gasping. 'I'm keen,' she said. 'Sign me up.'

Once Gemma agreed to join them, Sam left. They would practise every morning and afternoon, Denise explained.

Denise proved to be both a capable and effective teacher. Once she'd satisfied herself that they'd grasped the basics, she aimed to make their reactions instinctive. After that, even when they were swimming a stealthy arm might clutch at an arm or ankle and Alice's responses grew swifter as the days passed.

'Assailants will mostly be male, but not always,' Denise explained after one spirited session, pausing to let them catch their breath. 'Remember, girls generally attack in groups. Practise each new move every day until you can rely on your muscle-memory as well as your intuition. Plus keep reminding yourself of all the usual safeguards, until they're part of you.'

She numbered them off on her fingers. 'Keep your head high and meet people's gaze so they know you've seen them. Walk confidently. When you're walking alone, remove your earphones so you're alert to odd noises, to being approached. Always buy or pour your own drinks, and don't leave them unattended. Write down the number of any taxi you get into. Have your keys handy before you approach your car, don't stand and fumble. And if in trouble yell, Fire! rather than Help! People respond better,' she chuckled.

Gemma gulped. 'Did you want to say something?' Denise asked, but Gemma shook her head.

One afternoon, Sam joined them, saying she needed some practise. Was something bothering her? To Alice's eyes, she looked tense and she didn't stay long.

Gemma appeared a bit off-hand about the training but Alice couldn't get enough of it. She surprised herself by being quick on her feet and a fast learner. The physical contact revived some hidden memories, she'd expected that. But as she overcame her 'attackers' time after time a dark delight grew, primal and deep.

During a routine with Denise one afternoon Alice took an unexpected tumble, finding herself prone on the mat for a few seconds, slightly stunned. The old nightmares flooded through her and she scrambled to her feet, blind with rage. Lashing out wildly at unseen figures, she knew she could now punch, kick, smash them to the floor because for once, she wasn't alone. She came to her senses to feel Denise restraining her, holding her arms.

'Alice, what is it?' she demanded. 'Anger's okay, but this is way over the top. What's going on?'

Alice glared back, scarcely seeing her. Wrenching herself free, she punched at the sofa cushions instead, hearing choking, guttural sounds come out of her mouth. Then the tears came.

15

GEMMA

Gemma gaped at Alice, punching at cushions and crying like a kid. Cool, calm, scientific Alice. What had brought this on? Was she having a fit?

Her mind raced through their conversations, Alice speaking about her dreary life at home, about Tracey's devotion to her sons, her own loathing of her brothers. Her various hints about choosing to get fat. But why? Why would anyone so attractive do that?

No, surely not? Yet even as Gemma hesitated, her unease about Alice's brothers rose up. It was something to do with them.

She raced to Alice's side. 'Give this game everything you've got,' she said, patting her clumsily and handing over some tissues. 'Don't give up. One day you'll get those brothers where it hurts. You will!' The red-rimmed eyes filled with panic. 'It's okay,' Gemma urged, trusting her instincts, 'Go for it.'

Understanding of some kind passed between them and relief flooded into Alice's face, bringing a watery calm. She stood up and shakily mopped her face. 'Bad memories,' she mumbled to Denise and Gemma as they embraced her. 'Sorry, need a walk.'

Denise lifted her shoulders in enquiry but Gemma shrugged. She'd acted on gut feeling. Only Alice knew what brought on that rage, but if it was her brothers they'd better watch out. Alice meant business.

Denise excused herself to go and work on the plane. She'd stay and have dinner with her friends, she said. Could Gemma tell Sam and check on Alice?

Gemma ran for the beach but couldn't see Alice. Back at the house, in response to Sam's questioning she said, 'I think it's family stuff.'

'Bad memories?' Sam mused. 'Violated boundaries perhaps. Anger like that can signal there's been a serious breach somewhere. It's painful to remember, especially if we've blamed ourselves for letting it happen.'

Her tone suggested she'd be okay with whatever happened. Was the woman bulletproof? Gemma couldn't shake off the image of Alice beating her fists on the sofa, an echo of her own rage on the beach. She paced around the house with her sketchbook, unable to draw or concentrate on anything until Sam called her into the kitchen to help with the meal.

It seemed ages until her cousin came back, sandy and dishevelled but calm. It's the beach, Gemma marvelled to herself. There's something about being alone with just the sea and the sky.

No one pressed Alice to speak, but over dinner she

made it clear she'd returned with her new, upbeat humour to the fore. Gemma liked that she no longer made caustic jokes at her own expense. The anarchists too had never tired of their smartass cynicism and Gemma couldn't believe that she'd ever laughed along with them.

As they ate, Alice gave an impromptu performance of a child reciting 'What I did in the holidays.' Based on their time with Sam so far, her recital ranged from a meeting a gypsy who could be a witch to flinging first her cousin, then her host and finally her instructor onto the living room floor.

'I didn't want to come here, you know that,' she said to Sam as they stopped laughing. 'I was certain you were another of my mother's do-gooder shrinks. I didn't trust you. How could I? I didn't trust myself.' She gulped down her iced water and Gemma sensed the determination behind her humour.

'What you said to me earlier,' Alice turned to her, voice still steady. 'You've guessed what my brothers have done to me? And their friends?'

Gemma stared back, feeling her face rigid with distress. She couldn't find any words.

'I did what I could to stop them,' Alice held her gaze, as though trying to find a way into her mind. 'But three against one, sometimes more, they were always stronger.'

She turned to Sam, her voice calm, her tone cool.

'After a while, getting fat and ugly seemed my one hope of stopping them, of keeping myself safe.'

'You're speaking of abuse, Alice?' Sam leaned across the table and gently took her hands. 'Sexual abuse?'

Alice nodded, lowering her gaze.

'When did it start?'

'When they came home from boarding school, after our father disappeared. I was five. It got worse later.' She glanced up at Sam, withdrawing one hand to crumble some bread onto her plate. 'I expect you know about Dad?'

Sam nodded. 'A bit. But you, Alice, what happened? Can you say?'

'Mostly touching. They said it didn't count, but I didn't believe them.'

'It's abuse,' Sam's voice remained quiet but firm. 'You were right. Never doubt it, Alice. And your mother? Or did they threaten you if you told Tracey? Frighten you?'

Another nod.

'You mentioned their friends?'

'They came after a while. They – they looked. My brothers held me down and they paid to look. It cost more to touch.' Her face twisted with pain.

Tears running down her cheeks, Gemma ached at such callous cruelty to a little girl yet Alice remained dry-eyed.

'Oh, Alice, ' Sam breathed. 'All these years? You told no one?'

Alice moved her head almost imperceptibly.

'Has it stopped?'

Alice attempted a ghastly smile. 'I made it stop. They still treat me like dirt but – not that.'

A long silence followed. Gemma's fingers were white from gripping the arms of her chair and she unclenched them.

'Anything else, Alice?' Sam asked.

'They called me names,' Alice shuddered. 'I know I shouldn't care, they're only words, but I do. And they said because the other wasn't actual – you know – that it didn't matter, was nothing, zero, zilch, wasn't even wrong.'

Behind her frozen expression, Gemma sensed a white-hot fury.

'But I hate them,' Alice clenched her fists. 'I didn't know how much until I pictured smashing them down on the floor today, one by one. Because they – it stopped, I thought it was over but I'd stuffed it down.'

Gemma saw Sam's expression harden. 'All that rage.'

'I'm glad I told someone. I've been trying to get over it but I can't, even though things are different now.' Alice spoke like someone trying to convince herself.

'Not so different, Alice,' Sam spoke wearily. 'Verbal abuse, sexual, physical, emotional abuse, it's all cruel, violent and vicious. You shouldn't have to endure it, especially not in your own family. No one should.'

She lapsed into silence while Alice sat like a stone.

'You know you have several options, Alice?' Sam said, after a long pause. 'Speaking to your mother on your own, or with someone else present?'

Alice shook her head vehemently and rubbed at her eyes.

'No? Then there's making a formal complaint? There are sexual violence authorities that can help you,' Sam offered. 'You're strong Alice, but it's not weakness to ask for help.'

Alice recoiled. 'Never! I've had enough of authorities. And it would destroy Tracey – if she believed me. No, she mustn't know yet. Maybe when we've all left home?'

Recalling her aunt's well-known hysterics, Gemma totally got that Tracey wouldn't be much of an ally. 'You could leave home now,' she suggested. 'Leave the lot of them. There are allowances you can get, you could go and study somewhere. Do science, do botany, like you want to.'

'I want to set things straight first.' Alice rubbed at her elbows where they rested on the table. 'That's what I've been thinking about on the beach. Too many boys get away with stuff like this. Even when the authorities do get involved, they focus on the women. Mud sticks to them, not the men.' She turned to Sam. 'It's like you said, men make the rules and then they judge. And they've already decided on the outcome. But not this time. Not with me. Not any more.'

'What are you saying?' Sam queried. 'What do you want?'

'I want some old-fashioned revenge,' Alice grinned, more of a grimace than a smile. 'Legal but painful. Preferably excruciating. Administered by me. Anonymously.'

She actually laughed then; Gemma flinched at the sound.

Sam studied her. 'Say more?'

Gemma strained to hear Alice's answer. 'I'm going to punish them. I don't know how, but I'll work it out. You can't talk me out of it. I'll be careful,' she insisted, in response to Sam's quick intake of breath. 'They'll never suspect me, they're convinced I'm still scared of them. After that, I'll get on with my life. I'm going to study botany, get a scholarship, do everything it takes to do science in the way Mikael showed us. '

'I'm sure you will. And maybe a little remedial justice would be constructive for everyone concerned?' Sam mused. She leaned back, turning to Gemma, 'Perhaps your father suspected something? Did he speak much about his nephews?'

Gemma shook her head. 'I didn't hear anything. Our families don't hang out much.' With Sam and Alice watching her, she added, 'I hated the way they looked at me, they gave me the creeps.'

Alice shuddered and gave a small moan. 'They didn't –'

'No, they never touched me.' But someone else had. Gemma pushed the memories away.

'Did your mother have any suspicions, do you think?' Sam asked Alice.

'No, how could she? But she talked a lot about Gemma's dad recently,' Alice spoke more freely. 'She said something about him being a good brother, because he paid for me to come here, I suppose. I doubt she'd have bothered sending me, if she had to.'

'Would she give herself a holiday?' Sam asked.

Alice reddened, shook her head. 'Everything's for the boys.'

'If she does everything for your brothers, she's trying to bind them to her,' Sam murmured. 'So they won't leave her, like your father did.'

16

ALICE

The next day, Alice found Sam on the beach enjoying an early morning coffee and sat down beside her. Sunlight reflecting off the water stung her sore eyes and the smell of Sam's coffee caught at her throat. She'd spent much of the night rehearsing this conversation and her head ached. Sam half turned towards her, still looking out to sea.

'I don't understand your game, but thanks for being okay with me last night,' Alice burst out. 'I'm not ready to talk any more about – my brothers. You're the first people I've told but I don't want to even think about it for now.' She gestured at the scene around them. 'It feels like a waste. I might never get a chance like this again.'

Sam nodded. 'Is that because something else matters more?'

'That's it.' Alice's shoulders relaxed. 'Something else matters more. This chance, the beach, everything.' She waved a hand. 'I don't want them here ruining it, when I'm finally away from them. Gemma understands. She's okay if we leave it.'

Sam put down her coffee and gave her a quick hug. 'Me too,' she said. 'You'll get past this, if that's what you want, Alice. You're strong. Thanks for trusting us. And yourself.'

Alice considered. Could she do it? Drop a lifetime's resentments? Her chin lifted, prompting memories of Lise Meitner and the violations that could have ruined her life. The recollection warmed her. Was there something to this game after all?

Alice returned to the self-defence classes. Denise produced a small punching bag, borrowed from the farmer's son, and showed both girls how to use it. 'Perfect for letting off steam,' she advised, and Alice relished the thump of her fists as they connected with hard leather.

Some days later, their defensive skills mastered to Sam's satisfaction, they gathered at the farm's airfield to farewell their instructor.

Alice watched the little plane leave with mixed feelings, remembering her collapse. Sam had called it being vulnerable, saying it needed a special strength. Being called vulnerable and strong at the same time felt paradoxical – but Alice wouldn't try and work Sam out any more. She'd enough to do keeping up with her game, the woman was unstoppable.

After the sound of the plane's engines died away, Sam

took them to one of the outbuildings, unlocking it to reveal a well-equipped workshop.

'Carpentry's next in the Game. I'll teach you myself, if you're willing,' she said, pointing out a range of power tools, including an impressive drill and some electric screwdrivers. 'I'll show you how to use all these. I'll also make sure you can manage a hammer, saw and ordinary screwdriver as well, and do basic carpentry,' she added. 'Woodwork's a skill that everyone needs. Gemma, you'll work with stage sets. Think how useful this will be.'

Gemma beamed at Sam's certainty that she'd work in theatre one day.

Alice considered the changes in her cousin since seeing that strange play. Sam had already found a young playwrights' competition at a Performing Arts college, and Gemma worked on her entry every spare moment. After the holidays, she planned to return to school and persuade her parents to let her change courses. She'd do it too. If only her own future could be so clear.

Later the next morning, Alice surveyed the set of brackets she'd just fixed to the workshop wall, feeling absurdly proud. 'I can't see how I'll use carpentry, but it's not so hard,' she told Sam.

'Making shelves to hold your botanical specimens? A hidden trapdoor as part of some exquisitely painful remedial justice?' Sam offered, giving the brackets an experimental tug and pronouncing them secure.

'Now *that's* tempting,' Alice relished the joke. Power tools made building so easy; she'd persuade Tracey to buy an electric screwdriver at least.

They worked through several projects, Alice enjoying the feeling of timber in her hands. To Gemma's amusement, she examined the grain and smelled each piece of wood she handled. She even hummed to herself as she sandpapered sharp corners into smoothness.

When they'd completed their list, Sam joined them, helping put away tools, wood scraps and sweep up sawdust.

'We've gained some shelves, a storage rack, a new compost bin and a mended bird feeder,' she said with satisfaction. 'Well done, both of you and thank you. But the main thing is you've got new skills; you never know when you'll need them.'

'Have we earned a rest?' Gemma gave her a cheeky look as they left the shed.

'Until tomorrow,' Sam pushed back her hair. 'Someone else is coming to show you something I'm certain you've never been taught. And it's important – '

'For Sam's-Game-whatever-it-is,' Alice and Gemma chorused together, prompting a chuckle.

'Can you give us a clue?' Alice asked.

'You'll never guess. It's motor mechanics,' Sam told them, laughing at their expressions. 'Figuring out how a vehicle works isn't difficult and knowing a few simple tricks can get you out of all sorts of difficulties. You already drive, don't you?' she asked Gemma.

'And before you ask, I couldn't change a wheel if I had to,' Gemma admitted.

Alice would learn to drive, she decided there and then.

'If I had my way, I'd teach you both to fly as well,' Sam sighed. 'I'd my full pilot's license by my twenty-third birthday and I've kept my hours up since then. It meant I could fly emergency supplies into Bosnia in the 'nineties. Those are the moments you're glad of every survival skill you've been taught – '

She waved away their questions. 'It's not a topic to talk about today, far too many atrocities. The tide's full, enjoy your free afternoon.'

The following morning a tall, blonde woman arrived on a motorbike. Ingrid would teach them basic vehicle maintenance and the principles of motors.

'I was lucky enough to do my apprenticeship with a woman who owned a sports car garage,' she told them in her husky voice. 'She'd trained at the Grand Prix community in France. By the time I met her, Sybille was a legend in the racing world. When it came to getting extra power out of their engines, the drivers hung on her every word.'

She unpacked her pannier bag and handed each of

them an overall. 'Sybille worked into her 'seventies before selling her business to us, the three women who'd been her apprentices. We still look after some of her clients while she retired to a Pacific Island to enjoy a disgraceful old age.'

'I hope she took different clothes?' Alice held up the voluminous garment. 'How do I get into this?'

As she suspected, mechanics was messy work. Their hair secured under shower caps, they endured long, sweaty periods under, inside and bending over Sam's red vehicle.

Ingrid mixed her instruction and information with a stream of cheerful chatter. As she talked, she demonstrated the easiest way to manage heavy tasks and the many greasy processes. By the end of their brief apprenticeship, both Alice and Gemma could change a wheel, check oils and fluids, belts, coolants and more. They understood the basics of an engine and the purpose of every light on a car's dashboard, or control panel as Ingrid called it.

Alice liked the precision of the motor's parts, how they'd been machined to fit perfectly together yet still moved.

'Most people just notice a car's shape and colour,' Ingrid agreed, 'Not many appreciate the engine.'

The salty breeze tasted delicious on the morning they

finished their last sticky encounter with engine oil. Watching Ingrid roar off on her bike, Alice stretched her aching back. She longed to relax.

'Let's have the rest of the day off,' Sam had joined them towards the end. 'I'd like a long swim and then a rest with a book.'

Did Sam service her own vehicles and Apsara's motor too? Alice wouldn't be surprised.

Alice changed and slid gratefully into the sea. Settling into a steady stroke across the bay, she idly thought of her twelve women. Could many of them swim? What would they make of this scene? A middle-aged woman in a scarlet bikini, swimming strongly and already halfway to the island? A young woman in black wearing a black fedora, scribbling in a notebook – Gemma, working on her script. And me in my sensible, one-piece bathing suit, powering back and forth across the bay while there's still time?

No, don't think about endings, she told herself. This moment's enough. It's perfect, and *that's* what the women would recognise and value.

The next day after a late breakfast, Sam opened a cupboard and produced a sewing machine, scissors, pins and a large box crammed with fabric, buttons, ribbons and braids. She set everything out on the table. 'Today it's sewing skills,' she informed them.

'Do we have a choice?' Alice had never used a sewing machine before. Tracey had tried to show her how but she'd refused.

Gemma jumped at the chance. 'I can make costumes,' she cried. 'Sewing wasn't an option at any of my schools.'

Alice associated sewing machines with sweatshops and women toiling for a pittance. 'Not for me thanks.' But Sam considered sewing an essential skill for them both, so along with Gemma, Alice learned to thread up the machine, fill and fit bobbins and try out various stitches. Twirling the dial for various patterns and stitching effects soon lost its appeal and she persisted only until she could make a passable pillowcase.

'Isn't that enough?' she implored Sam. 'I can mend fabric and hem a curtain now, why else would a botanist need to sew?'

'You could take in your clothes, or I could do it for you,' Gemma offered, looking up from her stitching. 'That skirt's way too big.'

Alice looked down. The swimming, walking and decent food was melting away the misery of recent years and the skirt hung loosely on her. 'Thanks, but maybe later? I might want a whole new wardrobe,' she said, hiding her surprise and pleasure. 'And so might you.'

She observed Gemma's efforts with her own clothes. She'd already sewn bright strips of cloth around the hem of one black tunic and transformed a black top with multi-coloured pockets.

'Genuine designer clothing,' Gemma announced as she adjusted the fabric. 'Designed by me.'

Sewing proved to be the last survival skill on Sam's list for them, but she agreed Gemma could go on using the machine, as a change from her writing.

'So what d'you think of the Game now?' Sam asked them the next day over lunch.

'Sam's-Game-whatever-it-is? I still don't know what it is but I've enjoyed your survival skills, most of them. Mechanics still bugs me, ' Gemma said. 'And I don't know why it's called a game.'

Sam nodded and turned to Alice.

'I don't know why it's called a game either,' Alice said after a pause. 'But I've had fun, even when things got messy. My twelve women already help me; none of them felt sorry for themselves, although their lives were hard.'

'Something else mattered more?'

'That's it.' Alice squinted into the sunshine.

Sam concentrated on stirring her coffee. 'You've met Denise and Ingrid,' she said. 'And Aishe. Would you like to meet more players in the Game?'

'Like you did, with Fran?' Alice asked.

'A bit like that, yes.'

'Before we decide, will you answer some questions?'

Alice spun around at Gemma's harsh tone.

Gemma leaned towards Sam, her eyes hard. 'What was that business with the graffiti and the seagull?' she demanded. 'What are we getting ourselves into?'

17

GEMMA

Gemma held her breath. Had she gone too far? Would Sam refuse to answer? She looked up from her coffee at last.

'You're entitled to ask and I'll answer, but I'll come at it in my own way. Can you be patient?' She waited for their nods. 'When you arrived here, I'd say you were both a bit earth-bound. If you'd been birds, one of your wings wasn't fully grown. You tended to fly in circles, somewhat unhappy circles. Is that fair?'

Gemma nodded. It sounded more than fair.

'That's the case with many girls who come here,' Sam assured her. 'So we go out, do different things, try new experiences. After a time, girls usually discover two things. What's been keeping them earth-bound and who or what inspires them. As you did. If they're willing to dig deep, that wing starts to grow. But do you think everyone's thrilled to see it when they go home? In many countries, it's forbidden for girls to shine, and even here there's opposition.'

'It's not the skills, is it?' Alice said. 'It's deciding to live what's best for *us*.'

'You've got it. Some families like the idea of their girls flying, until it happens.'

'And the seagull?' Gemma prompted.

'Yes, I'm getting to that. Not long ago, a professional couple asked me to help their youngest daughter. They worried that she'd no confidence and worse still, no ambition. They were concerned that she wouldn't have at least two university degrees by the time she married, like her sisters and other girls in their extended family.' She chuckled. 'Don't look so surprised, Gemma. Yours aren't the only parents with aspirations.'

'So what happened?' Alice asked.

'Once she could trust me, she asked to visit organisations that provide aid overseas. The women she chose from the box were all humanitarians. This girl admitted she hasn't a shred of interest in a career, a profession, status, even money. Finds the whole marriage market idea repellent.'

'What does she want?' Alice asked again.

'To help disadvantaged people. Not through religion, not through good works. She's just genuinely interested in people. It's already in her, all she's ever wanted to do.'

'What happened?' Gemma shifted in her chair. Sam was taking forever.

'She mastered the practical skills you've learned and more. Then returned home to say she was leaving school to do aid work overseas.'

'And?' Gemma could imagine.

'An uproar. I could almost hear it from here. After the dust settled they managed a compromise, with some difficulty. She's agreed to do a basic nursing course and then go abroad. Nursing's low-status in their social circle, and I'm not popular.'

'Being a doctor would have been better?' Gemma knew that type of family.

'She didn't want the years of study, although she could have managed it. There was a lot of pressure, but this girl with 'no confidence' found strength in herself to resist.'

'You'd think they'd be pleased, if that's why they'd sent her,' Alice scowled.

'Her older sisters especially were livid. They blamed me, wrote letters, said she'd disgraced the family, blighted their own futures and more. They threatened investigations.'

'But the seagull?'

'I'm getting there, Gemma. One of the sisters and her boyfriend were at that Jazz evening. He's a local. Remember the young people who came in late?'

Gemma did.

'They sat near one of Lela's friends. She heard them talking about me. What I'd done, where I lived. She told Lela, who told Aishe, who told me. You were there.'

'The graffiti was theirs?' Alice asked.

'Yes, a young person's act. A warning from them,

with lots of expletives. It took some scrubbing off.'

'Killing a seagull though, that's disgusting.' Alice wrinkled her nose.

'They found it dead on the road and seized on the symbolism. 'This bird is you. We will bring you down as you brought her down, brought the family down, blah blah blah.'

'Did the note really say that?' Bile rose in Gemma's throat. 'How do you know all this about them?'

'The girl's mother found out and phoned me.' Sam exhaled. 'She explained everything and apologised. She's the matriarch, helped get her daughter here in the first place. She's delighted to see her youngest so lively. There won't be any more trouble.'

'The threats? Were you scared?' Gemma needed to know.

'I've had threats before and I don't like them. But I understand fear. It makes people do strange things. Some parents can't accept their daughters make their own choices. They're convinced I've brainwashed them.'

'When girls come here, does it often go wrong?'

'I'm particular about who comes, Gemma, I told you that before. Not because I'm fussy but if they're not ready, girls can't move on. Then it's hard for them.'

How does she know when girls are ready? Gemma daren't ask. 'You asked before if we wanted to meet more players.' She shifted in her chair. 'Alice has been straight with you, but I haven't. I don't want to meet anyone else yet. Not until you know about what I've done. You might change your mind about me staying.'

She told them everything then, her allegiance to Jacob, of following him and unintentionally betraying him. 'When I came here, I hated myself for being so naïve,' Gemma confessed as she finished. 'People were shocked at me being involved with him. My parents anyway. Like I'd gone insane and was a huge disappointment to them, but they'd be brave about it.' She wiped her eyes. 'All Jane and Henry want is to have me back the way I was before. They'll hate what's happening here. They'll blame you.'

'You discovering theatre?' Sam asked. 'And planning to turn your back on law?'

'All of that. They'll be outraged. Offended. They'll make serious trouble for you, because they can.'

'Forget about me for now. Say how it is for you.'

'I'm fed up to here with them.' Gemma's hand flew to her throat. 'Yes, they made things easier with the court. And school. But they did it so *nicely*, like they'd studied 'How to talk to your troubled teenager' in a book. Word perfect but never real. They won't let me talk, won't listen. I have to 'move on.' She mimicked her mother. 'But she's really saying, Move back, back to how you were when you were ten.'

'What would you like to happen with them?' Sam asked.

Gemma shook her head. 'When Alice talked of revenge, it makes sense for her. But I've been the problem, the bad daughter. Jane and Henry haven't exactly been evil and they've got all the power. I don't know what to do.'

'Then for now, think what your women would do,' Sam suggested. 'There's no rush to decide about others coming here. See what comes to you and use this as practice –'

'For Sam's-Game-whatever-it-is?' Gemma managed a smile. 'I'll give it a go.'

Only a few hours later and Gemma was ready to invite Sam and Alice to the outcome of her efforts. The afternoon had flown by. 'I've a brand new play to show you after dinner,' she told them.

'I sorted my twelve women alphabetically which made Aphra Behn the first one I looked at,' she explained when they arrived in the front room. 'She was a scandalous dramatist and right away I knew what advice she'd give me. *'Create a satire.'* So, sit back and relax. You're about to see *'Gemma's Revenge'*, never to be repeated or even written down.'

She lined up her props, three hats labelled Jane, Henry and Gemma and a wig she'd twisted into ringlets to resemble a Judge's headwear. Once she was ready, she took a deep breath and launched into her impromptu script. 'This is a courtroom. On trial are Jane and Henry charged with cruel and unnatural niceness to a daughter.'

Putting on her own hat, Gemma made her accusation: *Failure to provide relevant care, followed by excessive niceness and unrealistic expectations of gratitude and obedience.*

Alternating hats and voices, she played all three characters in her family drama. Leapt from side to side. Rapped out accusations and defence. Made objections, excuses. Changed voices with the hats.

Switching personalities wasn't easy and at times she got it spectacularly wrong, making her audience laugh even more. Voicing her parents' apologies and pleas for forgiveness was the best fun.

When all her grievances had been aired, mutual forgiveness begged for and given, Gemma donned the wig and became the Judge.

'Summing up, I can say that justice has been done today,' she intoned. 'The Polite Parents have been publicly chastised for their lack of Proper care. Publicly humiliated for their superficial Niceness. They have been seen to be Not Perfect, a Profound Punishment. They have heard and accepted these charges and apologised. The Defendant is gratified and satisfied, and this Case is closed.'

She pulled off the wig and twisted it between her hands. The clock ticked on the wall and the house creaked. The sound of the surf crept back into her ears and still she waited, feeling hot and sweaty and a bit ridiculous. Surely Alice would say something?

'How was that? Sam asked at last. 'How do you feel?'

'Strange,' Gemma admitted. 'I'd planned horrible punishments for them, prison or the stocks so I could pelt them with tomatoes. But a different voice came out of my mouth. I'd never meant to just talk to them.'

'So you made it up as you went along?' Alice gazed, open-mouthed.

'Kind of.'

'I know what I heard, it was very clever, very funny,' Sam said. 'Brilliant. But you? What did you hear?'

'How trapped I've been. And how tricked about their motives. They've helped me but mostly to cover up everything, not to understand or because they cared. I needed to hear it said aloud.' She replaced the black fedora on her head. 'I saw what they keep hidden too.'

'Say more?' Sam asked.

'Behind their controlled social niceness bullshit, it's spooky. A scary, vicious and miserable way to live, not what I expected.'

Sam exhaled. 'Well seen. And Henry? You played him like a child around Jane. Sulky, resentful?'

'He never wins with her, I don't know why he bothers to argue. Henry's uptight about everything, even being shorter than her. That's why he stands rigid as a soldier.'

'And you now?' Sam asked again.

'I feel like I've faced up to something in my own way, and I don't hate them anymore. That's all gone.' Gemma couldn't sit still any longer. She jumped up and hugged Sam and then Alice. 'Thanks for listening.'

Sam hugged her then drew back in surprise. 'You've lost your sharp angles, you were all bones when you arrived.'

'And your hair's different too,' Alice added. 'Lots of colour coming through, it suits you.'

'Look who's talking,' Gemma grinned, 'Alice, the Gypsy Queen.'

Alice's hair now swung in a dark, glossy curtain down her back, secured with a bright scarf from Sam's cupboard.

'So Gemma, did I answer your questions about the seagull earlier?' Sam asked. 'You understand that things don't always go well here, so how do you feel now about meeting new players?'

'Bring them on,' Gemma rubbed her eyes. 'But not just yet, I'm wiped out. I'm going for a walk.'

18

ALICE

Alice watched Gemma leave. Was this what 'playing something out' meant?' Would her own revenge leave her with the same light feeling? Had others around Sam done anything like this?

'The players in your game,' she asked Sam, 'Are there many our age? Around here?'

'Some, yes. A few are studying or working further away. It depends on where they're up to with their lives.'

'We're both edgy about going home and the fights we'll face. Their stories could help.'

'I'd never let you leave here without others to help you, Alice,' Sam's face creased with concern. 'There are many women waiting to meet you both, offer support. In a day or so we'll have people arriving, some for a short visit, others will join us for meals. If the weather holds, we'll have a picnic. They'll all answer your questions, so think about what you want to ask.' She stretched and yawned. 'You'll make a list before you go too, five practical things to get you started on making changes. Don't worry, you'll be fine.'

'I'll need a new notebook then?' Alice grinned.

When the initial carload of women arrived to meet with her and Gemma, Alice's first and most disconcerting revelation was their deep respect for Sam. They spoke of her not as Sam or even as Samantha but as the Fire Keeper.

'She's a legend,' an older girl told them. 'Players gave her that title years ago. It's a rare privilege to be named a Fire Keeper, an exceptional honour. She'd never claim it for herself.'

'Lots of women wouldn't be around if it weren't for the Fire Keepers,' another woman chimed in. 'I've heard this tradition is hundreds of years old but the Game can only ever be played face to face.'

'And with those who're ready,' the first girl concluded. 'Not that it always feels that we're ready. I remember how sulky I was when I first came here.' She grimaced at the memory.

'Did you already know about these – Fire Keepers?' Alice's dismay cut deep. 'I'd no idea that's who Sam was.'

'No, I was too wrapped up in my miseries,' the other smiled. 'Everyone arrives a bit grumpy though. If we were satisfied with ourselves, we wouldn't come, would we?'

Should Alice ask what the title meant? She smiled to herself at the absurdity of the idea. She already knew.

How many times had Sam spoken of fire, the need for it in a person, the strength and the joy of it? The title was perfect for her. And what did that make her and Gemma? The Fire Keeper's girls?

A flush of delight rippled through Alice as the past weeks sprang into focus. How subtly Sam had drawn her and Gemma out of their despair to see their fears and glimpse their own fire at the same time. She'd helped to feed this fire in so many ways, yet let them grow into it their own time. Oh, Sam was a Fire Keeper all right. How lucky they'd been, having these weeks with her. And now they were meeting other women that she'd helped.

Alice and Gemma met countless players over the next few days. Young and old from varying nationalities and backgrounds, they called in to linger over long lunches, take walks or swim. Occasionally they met in cafes, parks or restaurants and all openly shared their stories of the Game, not glossing over the challenges yet clearly relishing their current lives. Alice's notebook filled with their contact details and answers to her questions and she soon asked Sam for a new one.

Some women kept in touch with each other and others chose not to, she found. These weren't social groups with the usual hidden rules. What they all did was support new players, when asked.

No topics were off limits. Gemma's late night mimicking of one elderly sophisticate had Alice shrieking with laughter. 'Heroin?' the white haired matron had declared. 'It's only one or two hits to addiction, sweethearts. Beware of silver foxes with nose candy, they don't have your best interests at heart!'

At the promised picnic, a dreadlocked woman approached Alice and introduced herself as Natalie. 'The Fire Keeper suggested I tell you about my research and the work I do now,' she said. 'I don't know why and don't need to know, but you can ask questions if you like.'

They sat on the grass and Natalie explained that she began her career by studying sexual abuse within families. Alice's eyes widened as she listened.

'Most abuse is by someone known to the survivor and I explored the role of culture in this,' Natalie said. 'By culture I don't mean race or nationality but social culture. Okay so far?'

Alice steeled herself to hear more and nodded.

'Our current culture is one where men who don't take no for an answer are tacitly admired, given status,' Natalie continued. 'Think of those mottoes – winners never quit and quitters never win. It's socially acceptable for a man to dominate and get what he wants, whatever the cost. I questioned the wider effects of an attitude like that.'

Alice shivered. 'What did you find?'

'This dominating, conquering approach is impacting on the whole earth, that's what I found. Even other planets aren't safe any more. Women buy into it too, not just men. Any culture that treats the world as something to be exploited abuses its mother, according to the ancient mythologies. So dominating females is widespread – look at the gender of most domesticated animals.' She wrinkled her nose in distaste.

'When I understood something about the attitudes behind abuse, it lit up what I really wanted to do. Now I work full time in environmental education – of myself, as much as anyone else.' She laughed and briefly outlined her current teaching career. 'It's the most demanding job, I'll never be finished and I love it.' Her eyes sparkled. 'So that's a bit of my story. The Fire Keeper said you're interested in earth sciences too? Here's my card if you ever want to talk.'

Alice took it and closed her notebook. Who could capture such a huge concept in words? She ventured another question, barely recognising her own hesitant voice. 'So what you started with, sexual abuse in families, I suppose it's not really personal when you see it like that?'

'It's no less abhorrent,' Natalie spoke firmly. 'In fact, I see it as even more hideous now, like a vile secret training ground for what's to come. Ending sexual abuse must be everyone's responsibility if we're to survive on this planet.' She flung out her arms. 'I could rave on about my work all day, but that's enough from me. Come and meet these three.' She pointed to a trio sitting under a tree.

'We're exploring the sidelining of women in science,' one of the group called out as they walked over. 'Women like us. Are you interested? I'm Sarah.'

Alice dragged her attention away from what she'd just heard and nodded. 'Yes, I've read about what happened to Lise Meitner.'

'Be warned, it still goes on,' Sarah shook her head. 'We three are all leaders in our fields. We're working on different international projects, but we still look out for each other and other women to make sure none of us are being sidelined. Not being told about a meeting, not invited to join a network, overlooked as a speaker and all the rest.'

'That's discrimination,' Alice objected. 'Employers can't do that any more, can they?'

Good-natured laughter met her words. 'The non-events are the hardest to challenge, that's why we have to help each other,' another woman explained. 'Not being picked for a conference or asked to be on a panel, not being asked to give a keynote address. Nothing's happened, so what's the problem? That's what we hear every time we raise these issues.'

Alice gasped. 'I'd never thought of that, thanks.'

She'd been told the same lie. Seeing Gemma beckoning from an empty picnic table, Alice made her farewells and went to join her.

'How's it going?' Gemma waved her notebook. 'I've got so much crammed in here and in my head. I can't fit much more in.'

'Me too,' Alice sat down. 'The smallest comment can change everything though. I've just had my eyes opened to something so obvious.' She passed on Sarah's last remark.

'Of course, your brothers insisted nothing had happened, didn't they. They must believe only full-scale rape is abuse, the morons,' Gemma paused. 'Does it help?' She sounded shy. She'd kept to their agreement and hadn't mentioned Alice's situation, but had clearly thought about it.

'I need time to absorb it, but yes. It blows my story wide open, makes it bigger. Even takes away a bit of the sting,' Alice heard herself saying. It was true.

'What about your revenge?' Gemma's face creased with mischief.

'It'll still be wicked! I'm bursting to wipe those smug smiles off their faces.'

'Want any help?'

'I'll do some planning on the trip home, keep you posted.' Alice tipped her head at Gemma's notebook. 'What's your best thing from today?'

Gemma opened a page and read. *'To be open to*

creativity, develop the constructive use of solitude.'

'That's good,' Alice agreed. 'I've heard a few crazy stories too, there's some outrageous women here.'

Sam joined them. 'Meeting useful people, you two?'

Gemma displayed the tiny sketches she'd made. 'Too many to remember, and I forget their names.'

'We could combine our notes,' Alice suggested. 'I've got most names, not faces.' She turned to Sam. 'Everyone's so generous, even answering questions I haven't even thought of yet.'

'Alice with no questions? Impossible.' Sam pulled a comical face. 'I'm enjoying seeing you both so full of fire.' She took in their stricken expressions. 'So you've heard?'

'About you being the Fire Keeper,' Gemma breathed. 'Yes, I'm sorry I didn't know. What should we call you now?'

'Fire Keeper describes a function; it's a great honour. But you can go on calling me Sam. Or Samantha if you're feeling particularly polite,' Sam spoke lightly. 'Just remember who *you* are.'

'The Fire Keeper's girls?' Alice murmured, earning an approving glance.

'Perhaps,' was all Sam said.

The visits ended by the final week of the holidays and Alice treasured every moment of those last few days. Sam left them to their own devices in the mornings, to read, walk and talk about what they'd discovered. They also kept up their swimming and self-defence practise. Alice hadn't been so fit for years and Gemma's parents might get a shock too, with their daughter no longer such a thin, pale waif.

While Gemma worked on her play for the competition Alice delved into botany, using both the computer and Sam's library. She tried out propagation ideas in Sam's garden and couldn't remember being so happy.

'Surely just one more question?' Sam teased Alice on their last afternoon. 'My days won't be the same without Alice's questions.'

'Just one then,' Alice ducked her head. 'Why's what you do called a game?'

Sam leaned back in her chair and laughed. 'Sam's-Game-whatever-it-is? The curly question last? Help me out then, give me some thoughts about the word Game.'

'Something usually shared?' Gemma suggested. She'd been thinking about the same thing. 'Enjoyable, not too serious?'

'*Being* game, not a victim. Being bold,' Alice added.

'Where you can have fun, but there are some basic rules or guidelines?' Gemma volunteered.

'In a game you can give your best but be playful about it. Not have to be competitive?' Alice put in, winning a smile from Sam.

'You learn to be open to winning and losing and still willing to take up a challenge?' Gemma came up with next.

'And it's used for prey,' Alice countered, 'Animals that get hunted.'

Sam nodded. 'Game has so many meanings, it's hard to pin down. That keeps it vague enough not to panic girls who're already nervous about coming here.'

'Like me,' Alice agreed.

'Do you think it confuses people trying to fit us into a category?' Sam added, 'And baffles opponents?'

'So it's a reasonable name for what you do here after all?' Gemma asked.

'We've never got past it, in spite of hundreds of suggestions. Players do experiment with finding new names. You're welcome to as well.'

'I'll keep to Sam's-Game-whatever-it-is,' Alice said.

'Although it's our Game now as well,' Gemma added.

'I'm flattered but don't spread that name around. I can't take all the credit,' Sam's eyes crinkled in amusement. 'Now, will you keep in touch with each other, and with me? By email, phone, any way you want? Tell us how things are going occasionally? I won't always be able to reply but I will read your messages.'

Lose touch with Gemma again? No way! And Sam? She was everything Alice imagined in a fairy godmother and she said so.

'Then as in all good stories, I'll grant you one wish each.' Sam reached into her pocket. 'You've both got contact details for players to help and advise you, but here's a gift for when things get ugly. Use it any time you're threatened or in danger.' With a flourish, she gave each of them a small package.

Alice and Gemma unwrapped them eagerly. Small identical cell phones blinked up at them.

'There's an emergency number already listed.' Sam showed them. 'You get one call each, don't waste it. Don't ever use this phone for anything else.'

Alice gasped. 'What sort of emergency? Is there something you know that we don't?'

Sam smiled. 'Nothing like that. But there'll be hazards ahead for you Alice, if you move into botany. Tracey won't like it, after what your father did.'

Alice stared. 'Why? What do you know about him?'

'What Henry told me, with Tracey's permission. That years ago he disappeared from his job in Brazil. That neither his employers nor her lawyers have been able to find him. Is that right?'

Since her birthday cards stopped coming and she'd been forbidden to speak of him again it was all Alice knew too.

'And you,' Sam turned to Gemma, 'I'm sure you'll persuade Jane and Henry to let you change courses for a theatre school. But it won't be easy and I suspect the plays you write will trigger alarm bells. And from what you say the anarchists are bad news.'

Alice regarded her with awe. 'Are you some type of Superwomen?'

"We're no magicians but players do have some influence in the world,' Sam admitted. 'And we cooperate. People can turn nasty when a girl takes up her life and soars, so that's why we developed this plan.' She tapped Alice's phone. 'One call, so don't waste it.'

'What do we do?' Gemma turned hers over and examined it.

'In an emergency, call the number. Say who you are, where you are, what's happening, what you need. You'll get help as soon as possible. You can mention my name,' Sam added. 'Players move fast and some have a lot of authority.'

'What if there's no danger but we still need help?' Gemma persisted.

'Your decision. In any case, certain people owe us favours and won't ask too many questions,' Sam said, smiling at them. 'And there'll be no goodbyes between us. It's been such a pleasure having you here, two new players – '

'In Sam's-Game-whatever-it-is – ' Gemma and Alice interrupted together.

PART TWO

19

ALICE

Alice dumped her shoulder bag on the empty seat beside her as the bus moved out from the transport centre. Not many passengers, good. She took out her notebook.

'You're not leaving, Alice, you're going somewhere – ' Sam's words as she hugged her goodbye. Words to plug the gaping hole inside her. How could she go back to – them? And yet she had to.

Her final list stared up at her from the open book. First, a new lock for her bedroom door at home to replace the old broom she jammed upside down under the door handle. Alice made a note – find Dad's tools, underlining the words as the bus cruised down the highway, away from the coast.

Tears threatened as she strained for a last glimpse of the sea. No more swims, no more stars at night. Just the same streetlights and smells from the takeaway next door. No more takeaways. She added that to her list too, along with Belts to keep her skirts and trousers from falling down. New clothes could wait. Her old ones would serve as camouflage in the meantime.

Restorative justice, she wrote, *Resetting boundaries.* She rolled the words around in her mouth. No more starting over while dragging her old victim self along, suffering, withdrawing, waiting for others to help.

'Live like someone who doesn't put up with abuse,' Sam's words again. *'Stay open – and move forward. No one else can do it for you.'*

Could she do it? Revenge herself and then drop her burden? Lighten up in the process? Even have fun? She needed data, Alice knew, solid, objective, scientific facts about her brothers, Species Horribilis. Mindless payback could easily misfire, make everything worse.

Players in Sam's game, what did they do about misogynists? Some moved past them, but others took action. Several of her own twelve women tried trickery, they had to. Alice liked Alexandra David-Néel's disguise during her visit to Tibet when the borders were closed to Westerners.

Disguise, that could work. She'd say she'd got eyestrain from too much sun and wear sunglasses all the time, the kind that made your eyes invisible. Pretend to read with them on and watch her brothers. They were used to her carrying a book around. She'd keep paper inside the book, make notes.

Feeling more cheerful, Alice called up an image of Dominic, not much older than her. She circled his name with her pen. Had they ever been close? No, it was always the three brothers – then her. What data did she have about him? Good-looking, vain, the shortest of the three. Great hair, he kept it thick and gelled. A mountain of glossy hair, to make himself look taller? Horribilis Target Number One would be Dom and his hair.

After Dom, Carl, her sarcastic middle brother, a walking, breathing stronghold of cynicism. Nothing escaped his righteous judgments.

And Brad? Not Brad, not yet. Revenge on Brad needed special planning. It had to hurt.

At home, a quick hug from Tracey and a few anxious words – 'You're feeling better? You've lost weight? We'll have a nice chat now you're home, and I must trim your hair.'

Alice had the sense of plunging back into a time warp where nothing had changed while she was away. How was it possible, when her own horizons had expanded so much? But her mother continued her long hours as a hair stylist. Her brothers filled their days with work, study and their own interests and even the same mess lingered in the TV room.

Alice began at once, recording Dom patting and smoothing his hair, glancing in mirrors to check the styling. On the bus, she'd dreamed up an imaginary school project involving genealogy. First she'd tell him about it, then 'discover' premature male baldness in their family genes. That would do for a start.

Where their father's hair was concerned, Alice held most of the trump cards. Their long-absent parent was last seen in Brazil twelve years ago, but even on earlier occasions when he'd briefly returned, her brothers seldom saw him. They were away in the boarding schools they'd attended since the age of five.

Little Alice survived alone in the midst of her parents' feuding, practising the strange words Daddy taught her and arranging his plant pictures.

During her father's rare times at home, the estranged couple used Alice to relay messages. She trotted from one to another, feeling both important and confused. 'Mummy says give me the letter she gave you to sign.' Or 'Daddy says meet him at the bank tomorrow at ten o'clock.'

She was five when he finally disappeared and like some vengeful Frida Kahlo, her mother scissored him out of every photograph in the house. She never discovered Alice's hoard of trimmings hidden under her mattress and Alice didn't tell.

So her brothers' memories of their father were hazy. As all mention of him was forbidden no one spoke of him, in her hearing anyway. It pleased Tracey to insist her boys resembled her side of the family, 'and wasn't that a blessing.'

Alice mentioned her genealogy study to Dom several times. He ignored her as usual, but she knew he'd heard. Then as he preened in front of the hall mirror on Saturday night, she passed by and murmured, 'You look nice, especially your hair,' before letting her face crumple in dismay.

'What's wrong, crybaby?' he snapped. 'I suppose you're sick of staying home but look at you, what d'you expect?'

'No, it's just – I'm worried about your hair,' Alice murmured, suppressing a giggle. He'd achieved a perfect pomp and it looked ridiculous.

'What about my hair?' He turned his head, admiring it.

'It's because of Dad.'

He turned and stared at her. 'What about Dad?'

'Don't forget he was already losing his hair when he disappeared,' she whispered. 'All the men in his family lost theirs early too. I've seen photos online while I was doing my project. It's hereditary, it'll happen to you.'

'Don't be stupid,' he said. 'We take after Tracey's side –' then stopped, frowning. Remembering their grandfather's shiny scalp, perhaps? 'Get out of my way, I'll be late.'

In his absence, Alice salted his precious boar-bristle hairbrush with black hair she'd been collecting from the household's combs and brushes. The next day, she glimpsed him scowling into the mirror.

From then on, every day she sprinkled a few hairs on his pillow, his brush and onto the shoulders of his jackets as they hung in the hall, even using fur from the cat.

Brad unknowingly helped by claiming that keeping his hair short made him look even more virile. 'It's the hairs on my chest that matter,' he bragged, flexing his biceps.

'Poor Brad,' she murmured to Dom after one such outburst. 'Do you think his hair's already – you know?'

She read from An Encyclopedia of Natural Health Remedies borrowed from the library when Dom was about. He was too lazy to look anything up himself.

A few days later, he flicked at the top of her head with rolled-up girlie magazine and muttered, 'Still doing that genealogy crap?'

She pretended to read, hiding her delight.

'That stuff about my hair, I suppose it's all rubbish?'

'No, it's genetics. There's some amazing cures for hair loss in here though – herbal tonics.'

'Herbal's natural, I suppose.'

'There are always hair transplants,' Alice added, getting a glare for her trouble. She turned some pages. 'The latest idea is caffeine.'

'What d'you mean, caffeine?'

'Have a look.' She jabbed a finger onto the page. 'It says here the caffeine in strong coffee stimulates hair follicles in the scalp, it's been proved to work.'

'That wouldn't be too difficult,' Dom mused, ignoring where she was pointing. 'I'll try it. And you keep quiet about this, unless you want a Chinese burn.'

Wincing at memories of earlier arm-twisting, Alice didn't add that scientists estimated sixty cups of coffee per day might indeed regrow hair but would also stop the heart. Dom deserved a few caffeine-induced sleepless nights. 'You rub plant-based stimulants into the scalp at the same time.' She gazed at him innocently, showing him the page again. 'A cut raw onion's the best. Then castor oil or fresh chili pepper. It's that easy.' He backed away in horror, eyes wide, mouth open.

Carl next. Alice spent a whole Sunday cataloguing his obsessive teeth brushing, hand washing and changes of clothing. As the reluctant cleaner of the bathroom she shared with her brothers, she identified Carl's problem easily. A hygiene freak, he feared germs.

Her mother never ventured into what she called the 'boys' bathroom', preferring her en-suite while visitors used the guest washroom. Alice devised a latex allergy that made her unable to wear rubber gloves, expounding on the diagnosis by a 'doctor at the beach.' Tracey agreed that cleaning the boys' bathroom without gloves was unwise. 'The boys can go on cleaning it themselves for a few weeks,' she said.

Alice knew that such cleaning never took place. It was already grimy after her time away. When she had the place to herself, she used a small paintbrush to insert fresh yoghurt into crevices around the shower, bath, toilet and washbasin, and between gaps in the floor tiles. She would give her fungal experiment optimum warm, steamy conditions. No more using the ventilator fan or opening windows from now on.

Within days the culture thickened into sinister black streaks and Alice changed her reading matter to a volume on Skin Infections. Finding Carl watching TV, bare feet slung over the arm of his chair as usual, Alice walked by, stared at his feet and then back at her open book.

'What are you looking at?' he snapped.

Alice sank down on the sofa, making sure to glance at his feet again, frown and read some more.

'I said what are you looking at, Fatso?'

Resisting the urge to thump him with the heavy book, she mumbled, 'Blastomycosis.'

'What did you say?' he snarled. 'Are you giving me lip, Fatso? You'll be sorry.'

'No, Blastomycosis. It's a skin infection, like jock itch or athlete's foot, only more serious. Starts with red patches.'

'Why read about that? Oh, don't tell me, you're such a swot.'

Alice shrugged. 'It's probably nothing but –'

'But what?' he sneered.

'Aren't there some red patches on your feet?'

He examined them. 'I can't see anything.'

'That's good, maybe it's these glasses.'

'Stupid things, I don't know why you wear them indoors.'

Alice returned to her book. She could be patient.

As the fungal patches in the bathroom expanded, she found towels carpeting the floor after Carl's showers. When the question of her latex allergy came up, she complained about swollen eyes and the bathroom continued un-cleaned.

'Are you sure it's an allergy you've got,' Carl demanded, cornering her one evening. 'You're not just faking it?'

'Yes, I had some tests,' Alice lied. 'I'm taking something for it. Why?'

'Someone should clean that filthy bathroom, we'll catch something from it.' He glanced at the book under her arm. 'What's it say about foot infections?'

Alice opened it to her bookmarked page. 'It says here the symptoms are slow to appear and very hard to treat. It makes the skin go red in patches, and then go white and smell like rotting flesh,' she read. 'Your hands already look awful.' Carl's hands were red and chafed from his compulsive washing.

He shoved them into his pockets and scowled. 'Mind your own business. That's why I don't use swimming pool showers, they're full of germs.' He hesitated. 'Since you're such a know-all, take another look at my feet. Properly this time.'

Alice overlooked the missing 'Please' and complied, noting the manicured nails and scrubbed white skin. 'There might be something,' she bent back his toes and scrutinized underneath. 'Some redness under here. Any tingling?'

'Why?'

'It's an early symptom,' she offered. 'Maybe you should get a doctor to look at them. What about – you know – jock itch?'

Involuntarily he scratched at his crotch. 'Don't be stupid, of course I haven't.'

'That's a relief,' Alice suppressed a grin. 'Because they're related. If you even get athlete's foot, it leads to – the other, if you know what I mean. That means antibiotics, lots of them.'

'I had enough of those things when I was a kid, they ruin your gut. There must be other things to do. Find something, since you're so smart.'

Alice read from her book. 'Here's the recommended natural remedy for fungal infections. Soak the affected area daily with dilute household bleach and avoid anything with yeast in it, especially beer and wine.' His appalled expression was her reward. 'Bad luck, do you want to read it for yourself?' Straight-faced, she offered him the book.

'Get lost,' he slammed out of the room. Bottles and packets crashed together as he rummaged in cupboards.

Later, she'd tell him about systemic fungal infections

like aspergillosis that affected the lungs and could spread to the brain and kidneys; or mucormycosis and histoplasmosis – but that could wait. Perhaps her future lay in histology?

Stroking the black cat on her lap, glossy from her regular brushing, Alice sent another email to Gemma and Sam enthusing on her progress in the pleasurable art and science of revenge.

That left Brad, the brother Alice feared the most. The last thing she wanted was to attract his attention, even thinking about it brought on a churning dread. But he mustn't escape, and as a scientist, she could still study him objectively.

Alice re-read her notes. *Misogynist. Crude about women. Craves sexual encounters to crow about. Hangs out with males impressed by his virility.* Everything is vulnerable, isn't it? Even virility? Alice turned to cyberspace, and yes, there was lots on the Internet about risks to male fertility.

Environmental toxins like lead and pesticides have potential to reduce male sperm count, she read. So did excessive drug or alcohol use and smoking tobacco, plus obvious causes like injury. One report caught her attention, the danger to testes of overheating from wearing tight clothing. So Brad's claim of being the hottest stud in town might prove his downfall.

Normally Alice threw all the male clothing into a

pile when she sorted the clean laundry. The next time though, she examined Brad's jeans. Unmistakable signs of wear and strain suggested they were too tight. Was Brad putting on weight since he no longer played so much sport? He hadn't joined many teams since dropping out of uni and getting his job as an insurance clerk.

Alice retreated to her room and locked the door. Even this much speculation about Brad tested her bravado. The smell of clean sheets and lavender-scented candles reminded her of Sam's and she smoothed her hand over her locked and polished desk. Hidden inside, her emergency phone waited. A total waste to use it over Brad, he wasn't worth it. She would think of something.

Alice stretched out on the bed, hands behind her head, musing over her summer. First Sam herself, then her own twelve women and the players they'd met, intelligent, kind, competent women who'd told their stories and answered Alice's questions about abuse.

'With persistent bullies when you're feeling particularly threatened, find a way to go above them,' one had advised her. 'Bullies are cowards, basically weak. They're super-quick to avoid blame from someone stronger and that shifts their attention away from you, gives you time to re-focus. So remember to sidetrack them whenever you need to.'

Brad a coward? It confronted all her terrors to see

him as weak. Yet Alice glimpsed petulance behind his loud-mouthed blustering. Did he resent his Man of the family role, as the eldest? Was he jealous of his siblings, still wanting his mother all to himself?

Tracey was an unlikely ally for plotting Brad's ruin, yet Alice added her to her list. Knowing how her mother could talk, she suspected she'd soon regret it. And even after hours of prattling to clients at the hair salon, Tracey managed a monologue a day with her new, attentive audience. Alice relived every hair crisis with her, every speculation about her mother's favourite TV shows. Impossible to make notes too, with Tracey's eyes on her all the time.

'You read too much, you'll ruin your eyes. How about a nice chat?' from her mother meant, 'Put your book away and listen to me talk. And talk, and talk some more.'

Beneath the chatter, Alice felt the full force of the anxiety that kept Tracey clinging to her sons, her fear of being abandoned again. Whatever the cost to herself, she'd keep them dependent so she'd always be needed.

In amongst her prattling, Alice also found the key to Brad's downfall, Tracey's craving for grandchildren. Grandchildren meant even more perfect offspring to boast about. Grandchildren meant she would be endlessly useful. Grandchildren were essential for a future where she'd be safe. Tracey had everything planned. These grandchildren would arrive at respectable intervals following her sons' dazzling careers and successful marriages. She'd even chosen some of their names. Her naivety was breathtaking, her her determination absolute. Would she tolerate anyone frustrating these plans? Brad, of all people? No way! It was time to introduce Tracey to the topic of toppling male sperm counts.

Although she'd been expecting it, Alice recoiled at her mother's screech. Flapping the page she'd just been handed, Tracey shrieked, 'This doctor says fertility in men under thirty years is falling worldwide! This country is one of the worst in his survey!' She drew in a sharp breath, her face purpling. 'What about my grandchildren? What about our men? What's happening to my darling boys?'

'Sperm counts in men are down by fifty percent in the past fifty years,' Alice soberly re-arranged her pile of pages. 'Not just in the young ones.'

Tracey glared at her. 'You shouldn't know about such things. Why do they teach these nasty facts to young girls at school?'

'If they didn't, you wouldn't know what I'm telling you,' Alice kept her tone reasonable. 'With three sons, I thought you'd want to know what we learn in biology. Men need to be sensible, that's all, take precautions.'

'I should think so too,' her mother snapped, then coloured.

'Giving up on drugs and smoking, cutting down on alcohol are a good place to start,' Alice hid a grin at her mother's discomfiture. 'But with Brad, I think you need to worry about something else as well.'

'Brad? Don't be ridiculous,' Tracey simpered, her voice coy. 'He's so manly, takes after my family. Yes, he drinks a bit and has the occasional cigarette, although he tries to hide it from me. But a mother always knows. No, Brad's the least of my worries, he can get away with a tiny bit of indulgence. What are you talking about?'

'Tight jeans.' Alice kept a straight face with difficulty and pushed another page across the table.

Her mother shook her head, then skimmed the paragraphs and frowned 'Is this true? His clothes are – damaging him? My poor boy! So many threats, none of them his fault, it's all terribly unfair.' She turned to Alice. 'Do they know about this? Have you told them?'

'No way! They'd never listen to me,' Alice slumped in her chair looking defeated and matched her tone to her posture. There was a lengthy pause before Tracey's response.

'You're right, Alice,' her mother sighed. 'They wouldn't, although you do try to help. Leave this with me, I'll work something out. But promise to keep me informed. Tell me everything you can find out to keep your brothers – healthy.' She pursed her lips. 'We'll have to be careful not to alarm them. It'll be our little secret, you mustn't say a word.'

A smile softened her sharp features. 'I already dream about my grandchildren, especially Brad's. Girls or boys, they'll look perfectly gorgeous, just like him.'

Alice waited until her mother had gone before pretending to retch. 'Perfectly *gorgeous*,' she muttered to Blackie the cat.

'Tracey couldn't resist starting on Brad straight away,' Alice reported in her updates to Gemma and Sam. 'I knew she would. Every chance she gets she nags him to wear the baggy jeans she's bought him. This week she's trying to make him chew three cloves of garlic a day, it's my latest remedy. After the green tea and broccoli diet. Plus she pesters him about his alcohol, smoking and drugs. He's freaked out. Such a baby. It's like a circus here.'

She paused. Writing to Sam and Gemma recalled her real focus. 'I could tell her about the impact on sperm counts of birth control pills in the world's water supply,' she added, 'But that's enough revenge for me. I've got better things to do. Glad you've enjoyed my stories.'

The entire household was in an uproar – Carl at war with Dom about his raw egg hair treatments and the risk of salmonella poisoning. Dom complaining about the smell of bleach in the house and no dry towels. Carl demanding Tracey employ a cleaner or at least let him use her bathroom. Brad scowling, subdued and surly, snarling at everyone. The three of them competing for Tracey's attention. Magnificent.

Alice let hypochondria take over. Pleading schoolwork, she made herself unavailable. The fun was finished, her boundaries re-set, first with herself and now with her brothers. She'd a scholarship to win.

She took on more study, making it known she aimed for a future in botany. At home, she restored Eric's vegetable and herb gardens and kept notes on her plant experiments. Over and over, she remembered the women who'd helped her and her spirits soared.

Alice counted on the family noticing her even less than usual, with their new preoccupations. She did her chores when everyone was out, retreating to her room to study when they came home. She cooked for herself and often ate alone, delicious dishes that she'd made at Sam's. Having tried one or two unsuccessfully on her brothers, she continued to prepare the fry-ups and roast dinners they preferred.

But as the weight fell from her, she could no longer completely disguise it under her shapeless dresses. She also sometimes forgot to keep up her timid act.

Brad was the first to suspect. 'You're looking mighty pleased with yourself these days, Fatso,' he smirked one afternoon, finding her in the kitchen. 'Enjoy your little holiday by the seaside, did you? What did you do, make eyes at the ice-cream man? Fall for a fisherman?'

Stay cool, Alice told herself. Imagine shrinking his jeans in boiling water. The prospect pleased her and Brad noticed.

'Something funny, Fatso?' he snarled, grabbing her arm. Without thinking, Alice leaned into him and twisted out of his grip, forcing his wrist up behind his back. It took just seconds. Shocked, she dropped it, unable to move or speak.

Silence. Then came a slow, sinister voice. 'So you've learned some new tricks? Maybe it's even you behind all this crazy health fad stuff? You've made a fool of Dom and Carl, but not me, oh no.'

He turned and glared at her but she held her ground. 'Have I got you to thank for the new lifestyle advice, little sister?' he mocked.

Face him down, Alice urged herself, remember Dolores Huerta. Unblinking, she stayed silent and Brad was the first to look away. Rubbing his wrist, he stalked out of the room and Alice subsided onto a chair, heart racing.

Boundaries, she reminded herself, you've just re-set some boundaries. Brad knows it and you know it. Nevertheless she was glad of the new lock she'd fitted to her bedroom door.

20

GEMMA

Gemma stepped onto the train in a trance. Surely centuries had passed since she'd travelled the same route to Sam's, oblivious of anything but her own misery? Who was more real, that Gemma or this one who appreciated the bright carriage, wide windows, the comfortable seats? Noted with pleasure her fellow passengers? A mind wiped clean like a windscreen after rain, that's what she'd been given.

She settled into her buttoned red seat, notebook in hand. Beyond the window, the last view of the sea rushed away behind tall hedges. All still there, the beach, Sam's house, the island, although she couldn't see them. As was the old Gemma, a reservoir for future characters she'd create.

And her Revenge play, how had it happened? How had so much hidden knowledge been pulled out of her? Understandings that she couldn't deny, even if they didn't match her old story. Understanding that behind her mother's rigidity, rules and resolute niceness was fear, not meanness. And if the life Jane had chosen helped her to feel safe, it wasn't vindictive to want that same safety for Gemma. Dumb, maybe but not cruel.

And Henry, stiff and dry as a stick, he'd cared enough to support Jane's resolve to send her to Sam's. He'd paid for Alice too.

It seemed unfair that in spite of all this insight, Gemma wasn't going to be 'back on track' in the way they wanted. She was still going to disappoint them.

A memory of her mother brought a splutter of laughter, earning her a smile from the little boy sitting opposite. She'd once overheard Jane's end of a telephone conversation with her sister, 'I accept it's a stage Gemma's going through, just a stage.'

Gemma planned to go through lots more stages, outdoor stages, stages in theatres, basements and draughty halls, as many stages as she could manage. Stages that would sorely test Jane's acceptance.

She got out her red pen. Time to re-read her script with her wiped-clear mind and find parts that needed re-writing, even if it hurt to change her words. She still had work to do on it. When Henry's text arrived that he couldn't meet her as agreed and please take a taxi from the station, she wasn't even bothered.

As the security gates closed behind her and the taxi drove away, Gemma saw the tall house with fresh eyes. The ultimate in minimalist modern décor, it looked plain and drab after Sam's colourful villa.

Her own room felt gloomy too. After flinging open

the windows, Gemma spent a few minutes practising until she could skim her hat and land it on a hook behind her door, like Sean Connery in 007. Her lucky fedora, she'd worn it most days.

Running down to the kitchen, she found nothing much in the way of fruit and veg. She'd make a list. Lists reminded her of her number one task, to call Beth.

Her school counsellor answered at once, recognising her number. 'I'm back, can we meet?' Gemma blurted out, 'I'm keen to make a fresh start, got heaps to tell you,' before adding perfunctorily, 'Did you have a good summer too?'

'Not as good as yours, by the sound of it,' Beth's familiar voice sounded amused. 'Same place, usual time, tomorrow?'

Relieved, Gemma took the kitchen stool to her room and standing on the top step gazed out her open window, enjoying the birdsong and late afternoon sunshine. She took down her black curtains, leaving the windows bare, then replaced her black duvet cover with a plain red one. She hung up her altered clothes in the wardrobe where they stood out against the unrelieved black outfits hanging there. Above her desk, she pinned the programme from the play they'd seen then and removed some old punk posters. Already her room reflected her new resolve. Beth would be pleased. Good old Beth, she'd become an unexpected ally and Gemma had taken advantage of her kind nature, she knew it.

With half an hour left before her parents were due home, Gemma re-read the guidelines for the competition, wishing she knew more about plays. Volunteering with a theatre company was one way to learn, but would be too late to help with her entry.

At the familiar sound of the security gates admitting the family car, she put down the pages. Her stomach lurched as garage doors opened and closed and car doors slammed – then she was running downstairs.

Their reunion caught everyone by surprise. As Jane and Henry entered the house, Gemma forgot herself and hugged them. Following a brief and somewhat stiff response, they both stared at her.

'Gemma, your face, your hair!' her mother gasped. 'And your clothes –'

Did she look all that different? Gemma twirled in her colourful top and patchwork skirt. 'D'you like them? I made them myself – well, not so much made as altered.'

'Very artistic,' Henry stepped back to admire her. 'And you've got a tan.' He bit off his words, as though expecting a rebuke. 'Good holiday then?'

'You both know it wasn't a holiday,' Gemma patted his arm. 'But yes, and thanks. Thanks for fixing for me to spend time with Sam. And for putting up the money. And paying for Alice too.'

Jane raised an eyebrow. 'So it went well?'

'More than well,' Gemma confirmed.

Over a meal of Spinach Ricotta Ravioli, microwaved according to instructions, she answered Jane's rapid-fire questions. Yes, she was sleeping now. The travel went well. Sam was fine, she took them on lots of outings. Yes, she enjoyed Sam's company. And Alice's. They swam, took the boat out, had a good time.

When Jane turned back to her food, Gemma added, 'I'm ready to go back to school, make a fresh start. I phoned Beth, we're meeting tomorrow.' Some instinct warned her not to mention theatre plans yet.

'You're feeling better?' Jane persisted.

'Yes, I'm feeling better.' A glance passed between her parents, a slackening of tension. Was this the magic phrase they wanted?

'Back on track? That's good.' This from Henry. And that was all.

Gemma had worried how much to tell her parents about her time with Sam. Even Alice asked what to say when they got home.

'If they weren't too interested before you left, don't expect much when you get back,' Sam remarked dryly. 'They've been busy with their own lives and just want you to be okay.' And she'd been right. Would Beth be the same? Want Gemma to be 'back on track,' no longer a problem?

'And your summer?' Gemma tried again, getting only vague responses about their work. In their air-conditioned offices, they'd barely noticed the weather. I was the same, she reminded herself, indoors all day with the curtains closed.

She gave up. 'When are you ordering the groceries? I'll put some fruit and veg on the list.'

The next morning, Gemma waited in the café, enjoying the bustle of people, warm croissant smells, the hiss and steam of the coffee machine. Would she write in places like this one day, until they asked her to leave or at least buy a second drink?

She jumped up as Beth entered and hurried towards her. 'You look well,' the woman beamed then stopped, pushing back her grey hair.

'It's okay,' Gemma hugged her. 'I'm not going to bite your head off. Yes, I feel great, thanks for coming.' Noticing Beth's appreciative glance at her skirt, she smoothed it down.

'How could I resist, hearing you're making a fresh start?'

Gemma paid for their usual coffees and they sat down.

'It must have been quite a holiday,' Beth said. 'Tell me.'

'I met some amazing women, tried new things, learned a lot. Had time to think about what happened. Make some sense of it,' Gemma burst out, earning a smile. 'I know what I want do now, what I need to study.'

She described the theatre trip, its impact on her and her new understanding of her lifetime's sketching. Then she explained Sam's encouragement and the play competition. 'I've made mistakes but I've moved on. It's theatre studies for me now, and I'm willing to work to get there.'

'Gemma, it's a delight to hear you like this. What do your parents say?' Beth asked as their drinks arrived.

'I – well, I haven't got this far with them. Seeing me last night was enough of a shock.' Gemma gestured at herself, grinning at the memory. 'It wasn't deliberate. My hair got lighter in the sun, and the face-mongery kept getting sand in it after swimming so I took it out and lost most of it.'

'Bad luck. But the skirt? I'm in shock myself that you're not wearing black.'

'I learned to use a sewing machine, that's all. It was fun. I practised sewing bits onto my clothes. No big deal.'

'You look so well,' Beth murmured.

'All those weeks with two awesome cooks? Who wouldn't?'

'It's still a transformation,' Beth smiled. 'I can understand your parents' surprise.'

Now for the hard part. Gemma badly needed Beth's support. 'I actually wanted to talk to you first. About school, to find out what's possible. Can I change courses? Get away from preparing for Law and into the stream for Performing Arts?' She clutched her cup in both hands, heard Beth take a deep breath.

'It won't be easy, Gemma. It means you and your parents persuading the Dean. You'd have new subjects to catch up on, extra work.' She hesitated. 'But of course you can do it.'

'If there's a meeting with the Dean, could you be there too? It's a lot to ask but –'

'You'll need to convince me that you mean it this time, Gemma.' Beth said, unsmiling.

Gemma deserved that; she'd already messed Beth around. 'If I finish the assignments I was supposed to do at home, will that help?'

Beth put down her empty cup. 'When can you have them done by?'

'The end of this week?' She'd ignore her script and work around the clock on them. 'I'll post them on the class pages by Friday. Three o'clock?'

Beth raised her eyebrows and made a note in her diary. 'Let's see after that. I've a feeling there's more?'

'Just one thing,' Gemma described Sam's idea of her volunteering in a theatre. 'I hoped you might know someone?'

'There are internships, but most professional companies take on drama students to fill those. That leaves amateur groups,' Beth frowned. 'I'll see what I can find out.'

'It's a lot to put on you at once,' Gemma apologised.

'But I've almost finished my competition entry.'

'When's the deadline?' Beth let out a relieved breath when Gemma told her. 'Why this competition?'

'It's Sam's idea, to start me studying and to test myself. I've worked on it most of the summer. Also it might help persuade Jane and Henry.'

'I wish you well. Just don't let it interfere with your school grades,' Beth got up.

'I won't,' Gemma left the café with her. 'I'll be so different at home now, there won't be any problems.'

But she'd reckoned without her mother.

'No, Gemma, it's impossible,' Jane hung up her keys and changed into indoor shoes, placing her black-heeled sandals side by side at the front door. 'Theatre might be a fun hobby but not a career. Not for you with your brains and talent. I can't let you waste your life on it.'

She'd been in the house for ten minutes, listened to all Gemma had to say and still hadn't made eye contact with her daughter.

So much for her prepared speech, and for listing all the benefits of a performing arts degree, Gemma fumed silently. A pity Henry hadn't driven back with Jane. Should she have waited for him?

'I see things differently after my time away,' Gemma persisted, keeping her voice light. 'I'm certain theatre's right for me. That's what my drawing's been about, all these years, I just didn't understand. If I can change courses, I'll work hard and get good grades again. I'm already finishing my overdue assignments –'

'I'm happy to hear it,' Jane interrupted with a tinkling laugh, smoothing her hair in the hall mirror. 'You'll need to apply yourself to catch up.'

When she finally turned to face her, Gemma registered the fixed smile and hard, bright eyes. 'It's a pleasure to see you back to your old self, Gemma. We're so proud of you, your father and I. You've made an excellent recovery. You needn't worry, they've held your place in the best Law faculty in the country. We know you'll do well.' She exhaled. 'A family business, it's what we've always planned.'

'It's what you planned,' Gemma retorted. 'I wasn't ready –'

'Gemma, we've invested a lot in this. We –'

'Well, guess what? The share market just crashed. Time to write off your losses. Make better investments next time.'

'Gemma, can't you hear me?' Jane's cool voice cut her off again. 'I said it's impossible. Please leave it. I can hear that you're annoyed –'

'And I can hear that you're annoyed too!' Her mother flinched, and Gemma moderated her tone. 'I understand that you fought to be a lawyer when you were young. I'm glad it worked for you. But law's not for me. It was never for me.' She glimpsed a fleeting frown before Jane's face resumed its glacial smoothness.

'I'd like you to show me your new cooking skills, Gemma. I ordered some of those mushrooms you were telling us about, they should have been delivered earlier.'

That controlled voice, cool manner and implacable veneer. The facade that served Jane so well in the courtroom, Gemma couldn't make a dent in it. No wonder Henry got frustrated.

Reining in her temper, she unclenched her fists. Round One to Jane, but there was still Henry. And Jane should be careful what she said, or even more of her words might end up in a play.

At ten thirty the next morning, Gemma entered Henry's office carrying his favourite coffee and some snacks she'd made, using her new cooking skills. He whooped when he saw her and turned from the images of a large, old bungalow on his computer. 'Conveyancing?' she murmured, putting down the tray. 'A new house for a client?'

Yes,' Henry took up his coffee.

'You'd be interested to see what Samantha's done with her villa,' Gemma added, wide-eyed. 'I expect she's doubled its value in the last few years. She says the whole town's expanding, there's a huge demand for properties.'

Henry brightened. 'Really?' He turned back to his

screen and spent a few more moments deep in Real Estate heaven. 'Lots of potential there for development, you're right,' he sighed.

'Maybe people there need a lawyer like you to advise them?' Gemma teased.

'Not a chance, a local firm has a grip on the whole area,' Henry gave a last, lingering look at two seaside cottages for sale and picked up one of Gemma's snacks. 'These are good,' he bit into it. 'And so is the coffee.'

'Not everyone can see potential in old houses,' Gemma continued, as though he hadn't spoken. She'd learned that trick from Alice. 'You're brilliant at showing clients how to do up their properties. Why don't you do it yourself?'

Her father stopped mid-chew and stared at her. 'But I'm a lawyer.'

'Are you? I thought you were a human being. Law's not a life sentence.'

He swallowed. 'You're mighty opinionated today, young lady, what's got into you?'

Dear Henry, sitting so upright in his chair. Soon even she'd be taller than him. 'This isn't about me. You enjoy seeing old houses restored. You've a good eye for them. It must be hard enough seeing them go to your clients. Much worse if they don't appreciate their possibilities.' She had his attention now. 'Just think of the fun you'd have, doing up houses. You'd be the best in the business, make heaps of money.'

Henry sighed. 'Your mother – no, I couldn't.'

'Promise me you'll think about it?' Gemma picked up the tray.

'Maybe,' Henry took up some papers. 'Now off you go, I've got work to do. Remember, I'm in the city every afternoon this month. You're fine here by yourself? Not long until school starts.'

Round Two to me, Gemma smiled to herself.

It took several mid-morning chats to get Henry talking freely and one more until he admitted he was weary of law. Litigation exhausted him. Conveyancing frustrated him. 'People don't see the potential in most properties,' he sighed. 'They haven't the imagination.'

'Couldn't you develop just one old house, as a diversion? Or would that be a conflict of interest?' Gemma poured Henry more coffee. 'I won't tell.'

'Property is an area I know well,' Henry mused.

'You'd be using all your skills. Just in a different way.'

'And what's in it for you, Gemma?' Henry grinned unexpectedly. 'All these delicious morning teas aren't only for my benefit. Spit it out. Tell me exactly why I should influence Jane to let you change courses. I'm not deaf. I've heard you and your mother arguing.'

So she told him. 'I must have done okay,' she wrote to Alice and Sam, 'Henry's agreed to talk to Jane. If he can persuade her to meet with the Dean, he says that's all it will take. He's got a plan, won't tell me about it but at least he's listening.'

It took some time until Gemma and her parents were summoned to a meeting at the school. The Dean smelt of peppermints, concealing something else? Gemma had never spent time with her before. Her parents must have spoken to senior staff about her earlier 'exclusion', was it with this woman? Gemma sidestepped the thought.

Her request to change courses with its carefully listed reasons lay on the table in front of each of the four adults. Her assignments were up to date so Beth was there too.

From her chair near the door of the large boardroom, Gemma couldn't hear the conversation and watched their faces instead. Would the Dean side with Jane or with Beth? Did she know about Gemma's part in Jacob's arrest? Did she want her gone from this élite school? At least Henry would speak for her, he'd promised that much.

Gemma didn't share his confidence and her fingers ached for a pencil and paper to ease her anxiety. Then she noticed Henry lean back in his chair away from the women, folding his hands across his stomach. Was he giving up on her already? Traitor!

The three women bent their heads towards each other, no doubt all airing their different views on what was best for her. Gemma couldn't bear to watch any more and stared out the window. She'd have to run away after all.

After an eternity of waiting, a loud cough from Henry brought her back into the room to see Jane pushing back her glasses, looking gratified. Beth was smiling and Henry's grin definitely smug. The Dean just looked dazed and confused.

The four adults turned to Gemma and the Dean mumbled something. Apparently Gemma was on track for drama school. Not knowing who to thank, she fervently thanked them all.

'Henry's a cunning old fox,' she wrote in her email to Alice and Sam. 'He explained that as soon as Jane scents opposition, she has to win. So he warned her the Dean had doubts about my ability to switch courses. That's all it took. Jane mounted a full courtroom defence and Henry sat back and left her to it.'

She remembered the scene and added. 'Jane won, of course, now she has to live with it. Says she remembers what it's like to be young. As if.'

Would she ever fathom her mother?

21

ALICE

Alice and Brad continued to avoid each other but that earlier brief encounter made Alice even more determined to get away from him as soon as possible. That meant winning a scholarship and she'd already pondered several with help from a vocational guidance teacher. Some provided tuition only while others added an accommodation supplement. A few included a living allowance as well. Alice prepared several applications to send when exams were over. She'd high hopes for two of them, both in botany.

Leaving her mother to fuss over 'her boys' and their ongoing dramas, Alice eased herself out of Tracey's orbit as well. She'd preparations to make, and high on the list were some decent clothes.

'When you fly away with your fabulous scholarship, you might want a new image,' Gemma had written. 'When you're ready, describe your ideal clothes and I'll draw them for you. After that, I've got some suggestions.'

A new look for a new life? Alice sighed with pleasure. In the summer, she'd enjoyed dressing up, but could she really re-invent herself? She took her Boho smock off its hanger and smoothed the filmy fabric. It flowed easily over her clothes now but she didn't plan on wearing it around home.

When she moved away, she'd need pants and skirts that weren't tight or tailored, she decided, practical and plain and absolutely nothing black. Plus a colourful tunic. That would do. She sent off the details and waited for Gemma's reply.

When it came, the sketches showed Alice in huge horn-rimmed glasses modelling various garments, a white lab coat prominent in the background. She loved each and every design.

'Jane supports a charitable trust called Dressing for Success,' came Gemma's reply to her delighted response. 'It's run by professional women. They re-cycle used workplace outfits, and donate them to women starting out or changing careers. Nothing's new but they're good quality. I'm not sure about your tunic, but the rest should be easy.'

They agreed that Gemma would invent an imaginary friend in Alice's situation. Then after she and Jane selected the clothes using Alice's measurements, Gemma would plead confidentiality and send them on herself.

'Jane knows all about secrecy, she'll understand,' Gemma wrote. 'A woman lent her a full corporate outfit for her first job interview years ago, when she daren't ask her own mother. That's where she and her friends got the idea for this charity.'

Alice liked it that Gemma and Jane were getting on better. As long as Henry didn't drop his bombshell about a career change for a while. Like her, Gemma still had a lot to do.

When the courier delivered the large box a week later, Alice's hand shook as she signed for it. Hurrying to her room, she locked the door and tore off the wrappings. 'Courtesy of Dressing for Success,' the label said and a hand-written note inside wished her well in her future career.

Quickly slipping out of her old dress, Alice tried on the items, one by one. Tops, skirts, pants, a jacket, a coat and even scarves. Gemma had done well. Everything fitted and could be mixed and matched as she'd promised.

A slim package lay at the bottom and Alice opened it with trembling fingers. Two Boho tops, one in peacock colours and the other in rose-coloured silk with black embroidery. They were beautiful. Their labels read, Designed by Gemma. Alice held them against her and looked in the mirror, eyes brimming.

Slamming doors and loud voices downstairs warned her that Tracey and Carl were home with the groceries. Hurrying back into her old clothes, Alice folded the garments into her suitcase and slid it under the bed, then flattened the cardboard box and pushed it in afterwards. Unlocking her door, she headed for the kitchen, head held high.

'Alice, there you are.' Tracey trilled, looking up from the shopping bags. 'Exciting news, Brad's bringing a girl home for dinner on Friday night. She wants to meet us, insisted on it.'

Alice raised one eyebrow. 'Did Brad tell you this?' That would be a first.

'No, silly. We met them at the Mall just now,' Tracey twittered. 'She asked me straight out if she could come and visit. Brad wasn't keen but he couldn't say no, not with her standing right there. They met at the Gym, fancy that!'

She moved about stacking groceries into cupboards, while Carl washed his hands at the sink.

'Oh, leave off, Carl and help me. We'll plan a special menu, Alice. You can make one of your salads.' Tracey glanced at her daughter. 'This girl, her name's Justine, she's very slim. I expect she watches her weight so use a low-fat dressing. In fact, make everything low fat.'

'Low sugar as well?' Alice couldn't resist it. Tracey adored sweet things.

'Well, maybe a simple dessert. I'll be home as soon as I can to help.'

I bet, Alice muttered to herself.

22

GEMMA

'Where had Gemma been? Why was she off school for so long? How did she score such a great tan? What happened to her hair?' Gemma's first day back at school for months and just as she expected, avid curiosity about her absence from her former classmates.

She'd been a witness to a crime, she explained. The whole thing had shaken her up. Court appearances took forever, so it was far easier to study at home. She described the courtroom in such detail that even the budding lawyers around her got bored.

As for the tan, she'd been at a remote beach all summer. Remote meant no cafes, no boys, no nightlife and the questions ceased as abruptly as they began. Thankfully she would soon meet students doing different things, drama, dance and performing arts. For the first time in ages, she looked forward to classes.

Nothing in her new course disappointed her. Gemma put her whole heart into her studies and rarely hung out at the Mall any more, using the money saved from her clothing allowance to pay off her new sewing machine. Her redesigned clothes attracted attention from her new classmates and she'd even got a couple of orders. Life was sweet.

The sun warm on her back, Gemma strolled home from the bus stop one afternoon, pondering her next assignment. They were to write about Wendy Wasserstein's Heidi Chronicles. She barely noticed the car slowing beside her until it stopped.

Recognising it at once, her spirits plummeted. No chance to run and nowhere to hide. She held her head high and continued walking.

A tinted window slid down. 'Hello, Jacob's Girl,' snarled a familiar voice. 'Nearly didn't recognise you, all tarted up.'

Gemma's voice deserted her; she could scarcely breathe. Why couldn't they leave her alone?

'You double-crossing scumbag bitch, did you think we'd forgotten you?' A second voice now, the eyes invisible behind dark glasses. 'After what you did? Getting Jacob arrested?'

'Cowards,' she wanted to scream. 'You ran away.' She turned to face the car instead. 'I knew nothing about your plans that night. You all lied to me, remember?'

'That's not a nice thing to say, Jacob's Girl,' the first speaker sneered,

'I'm not Jacob's girl,' she snapped. 'Just get lost.'

'Or you'll call the police? Again?'

'I didn't know – ' Gemma gave up. Why waste her breath? She'd been a fool, hanging out with them.

'We're keeping an eye on you, Jacob's girl. Now you're back from wherever you've been. We said you wouldn't get away with it. You'll see us again,' came another voice as the car moved away.

The same old threesome, she might have known. Were they mad? They were all forbidden to associate with each other. Surely someone would see them?

But most afternoons as she turned into her lane the three cruised by, taunting her from the open car windows. If she used a different route or delayed her trip they found her, stalking her like predators.

Because of Jane's work and potential fallout from hostile divorces, their house had rock-solid security. Henry added a night security patrol after the fire. Even so, Gemma fretted until the driveway gates closed behind her each afternoon and she could escape inside the front door.

The three seemed bigger than she remembered, more menacing too. They'd often boasted about their crimes but Jacob assured her it was all hot air. 'They're babies,' he'd said. 'Trying to impress me. They've done nothing, never lived.' He'd lied about other things, why not about this? Would they hurt her? Did they know Henry wasn't home?

Since their arrest, the three were technically

underage offenders on juvenile probation, supervised by officers who were supposed to make regular visits to their homes, school and other haunts. Should she find out their JPO's and make a complaint?

But how, without alerting her parents? Disturbing the precarious peace between them? And it wouldn't solve anything, the creeps would just find other ways to hassle her.

'We're not supposed to associate,' she tried one afternoon. 'Why make trouble for yourselves.'

'But we're not associating with you. Who'd want to? Just driving by. Wondering what Jacob ever saw in you.'

Gemma's throat constricted.

'Stupid little rich bitch, that's what he called you. Did you know?'

That hurt, as it was meant to.

The phone calls began after that. Random calls each afternoon to the landline that Jane insisted on keeping. Nobody there when Gemma answered but she could almost smell them listening to her fear. After the fire, she'd changed her mobile, Henry's idea. Dear Henry, smarter than she gave him credit for.

Food stuck in her throat these days. Every night, she woke at the slightest noise. Could they break in? Gemma found herself slipping back into her miserable dark hole.

After one particularly vile encounter with the trio she sank into a chair, dropping her bag on the floor. What to do? Every one of 'her' twelve women had been harassed and endured much more than name-calling. Rachel Carson had the vitriol of the whole agro-chemical industry thrown at her, but she'd had help.

Gemma shared her unease with Alice and Sam, grateful she'd someone to tell. 'I'm ignoring them but I've written down the car details and days they follow me. I'm also making a record of everything I can remember about the group,' she told them in her emails. 'Names, dates, places, Jacob's speeches, the leaflets I edited. It's a kind of insurance. '

'A reasonable precaution,' Sam replied, adding 'From someone so determined not to be a lawyer!'

Sam's teasing always cheered Gemma up. Alice's response she had to re-read several times to make sure she got it.

'I've just learned that ignoring someone activates the part of their brain that detects physical hurt,' Alice wrote in her careful, scientific way. 'It means they won't get the message that you want to move on. If you get caught up in their pain, you'll forget about moving on too.'

Gemma snapped back to the present. How many hours had she wasted fretting over that carload of losers? Her script? When had she last worked on it? In her room, she re-read the sheaf of pages. Still heaps to do. She put on her lucky hat. Would the words still flow?

After that, she devoted herself to the play, ignoring distractions, walking by the car as though it wasn't there. She avoided her phone, social media, TV. The script gripped her and day by day, her characters acted and spoke more naturally. She'd no way of knowing what the judges wanted, just felt compelled to write it.

Once she was happy with it, she printed off four copies for the judges and made one for herself. Then walking home after posting the thick package, she broke into a run. She'd done it.

When the cruising vehicle next pulled up beside her, Gemma managed to speak calmly. 'Hey guys, I get the message,' she said. 'You're pissed about what happened but it's over. I'm into other stuff now. Jacob's out of the picture, why don't we all move on?'

The three smirked at one another. 'That's where you're wrong,' the driver sniggered, after a pause. 'Jacob's not out of the picture and it's not over.'

Gemma stared back, puzzled.

'Jacob's still the man, even from the inside,' he boasted. 'The word is he wants someone outside to run his old business.'

'Yeah, most likely us. Especially if he hears we can light little fires, just like him. Maybe at your place?' the boy in the back seat chimed in, ignoring the others' attempts to shut him up. 'Frizzle you up in your bed for what you did to Jacob?' His slurred words suggested drugs or drink, or both.

'Leave it,' Gemma urged. She wouldn't show fright. 'Make a fresh start, while you can.'

'Got an extra good reason to fry you now. You know too much. Better watch out, Jacob's girl, we're everywhere and we're watching you. We'll get you sooner or later.' The ugly words hung in the air as the car accelerated away.

Gemma made it inside before her trembling legs gave way. Jacob, still messing with drugs? She fought to breathe. The news sickened her almost as much as the incoherent threats.

Should she call the police? But what could they do with only threats? Their ponderous processes, the consultations, the paperwork, everything took so long. Her parents then? But tell them what? That this had been going on for weeks and she'd been disobeying the Court by 'having contact' with the boys? By not telling someone?

And Jacob? When they'd first met, he'd blazed with his vision for a better world. In those days, he'd motivated so many people, not just her. Perhaps he'd even inspired her writing. Had he lost all that? Or did the old Jacob still exist somewhere?

With the questions came an idea. Crazy and a bit

dangerous, but it might get those lunatics off her case. Maybe even keep a few kids off drugs? But she'd need to move fast.

Before she could hesitate, Gemma ran to her room and took from its hiding place the emergency phone Sam had given her, along with her notebook and a pen.

One call only. She read her guidelines as she pressed buttons with shaky fingers and gave her name to the woman who answered, asking what help she needed.

'To get a some printed pages to a prisoner as soon as possible,' Gemma explained and gave all the details she had.

As the anonymous voice asked questions, Gemma pictured the woman racing through possibilities. Was that voices in the background? She strained to hear, impatiently hopping from foot to foot. One she got her orders and read them back, she raced to grab her copy of her play, scribbled a note to go with it and left the house.

23

ALICE

Alice couldn't avoid cooking for one of Brad's girls and would have to eat with the family as well. She'd persuaded Tracey into a plain meal of grilled fish, roasted veg and salads. Tracey would bring home one of her favourite fruit tarts and that would have to do. Her brothers could fill up on pizzas later.

She set about preparing salads. When everything was ready, she took off her apron and pushed back her long hair. Her new clothes beckoned like sirens from under her bed but she daren't risk wearing them yet. Best to stay as the frumpy sister, silent and invisible.

As the couple entered the newly tidied house Alice stood back, wincing at Tracey's shrill welcome. Brad hovered possessively at the door looking very pleased with himself, while Carl and Dominic admired his latest beauty. And she was lovely, Alice couldn't deny it. How did Brad do it?

Alice hadn't expected to recognise the girl but she'd been at her school, several years ahead. Exceptionally clever, she'd won an academic award. Alice searched her memory for details.

Recognition wouldn't be mutual, seniors rarely noticed juniors. And sure enough, Justine showed no signs of knowing her, which suited Alice fine.

The food was served and admired and Tracey ensured conversation flowed. Everyone outdid themselves in being affable while Alice replenished plates and accepted compliments on her cooking. Did all this play-acting fool Justine? Her brothers usually communicated in grunts, shoving their plates at whoever had cooked for more food.

Justine herself puzzled Alice. The girl must be smart, brilliant even, yet contributed childishly to the conversation with helpless shrugs and appealing looks at Brad. And the more inane she appeared, the more Brad preened. At last, Alice couldn't stand it.

'You were ahead of me at school, Justine,' she said. 'I remember you well. You won the award for Academic Excellence overall. The highest marks ever achieved, weren't they?'

Everyone turned and stared at her. Justine appeared dumbstruck while Brad glowered. He turned to Justine, 'I didn't know that.'

'It's a while ago,' Justine faltered.

Brad twitched in his chair. He'd the look of a small boy who'd just learned the truth about the tooth fairy.

'That's lovely. Have some more wine, everyone,' Tracey urged, 'Then Alice will fetch dessert.' She turned to Justine. 'I've pralines to go with the coffee,

I hope you like them.'

'Oh, I do,' Justine affected her little girl voice.

Alice stood up to fetch fresh plates. They deserved each other.

The next morning, Brad cornered Alice in the kitchen. 'What was that about, showing me up in front of Justine last night?' He loomed over her, smelling of garlic and Alice recoiled. 'Were you trying to make me look stupid?' he snarled.

'I thought you'd like to know more about Justine,' Alice parried, avoiding his glare. Typical Brad, assuming everything was about him.

'I know loads about Justine,' he leered. 'More than enough for what I want. And I know loads about you too.' His eyes were cold. 'Like what a little prick tease you were with my friends years ago.'

Bile rose in Alice's throat and she stumbled. She reached out a hand to steady herself. 'What – what?' she stammered.

'What – what?' he mimicked. 'I remember you showing off years ago, a right little slut.'

'Me? Showing off? You – you held me down,' Alice gasped.

'Just as well we did, who knows what you'd have done,' Brad sneered. 'It's your word against mine. Who would Tracey believe? You – or me?'

Alice backed against the wall, tears running down

her cheeks.

'And don't think Dom and Carl will help you. I'll see to that.' Brad's smirk faded into cold rage. 'Make any more scenes for me like you did last night and you're finished. I'll make sure Tracey knows everything.'

Alice escaped to her room, shaking so much she could barely unlock the door. Re-locking it, she sank to the floor. So much for bravado and revenge.

24

GEMMA

Gemma phoned Alice on getting her despairing text and heard the whole story. 'That's horrible, he's sick. Are you safe now? What are you doing? '

'I'm locked in my room.'

'Will he really tell Tracey? She won't believe him, surely.' Gemma heard Alice gulping in air.

'He won't, he's just letting me know who's in charge. Maybe that's why all I can do is think about Dad. He should be here. He should be in charge. I can't stop wondering about him, probably because of the trick I played on Dom.'

Gemma could hear how wretched she sounded. 'Have you called Sam?'

'I left a message, but I needed to hear a friendly voice right now. Thanks for calling me back.' Gemma caught the uncharacteristic quaver in Alice's voice. 'Can you distract me? I'm too shaken up to talk sense. Tell me what you've been up to?'

'It might not help,' Gemma hesitated. 'It's been chaos here too, I was about to email you both. I used my wish yesterday, Sam's gift.'

'Your magic phone call?' Alice cried. 'What's happened?'

Gemma explained about the threats, and what she'd done.

'Wow, that's scary. You believed them? You must have, to take such a risk. I hope it works.' Alice spoke in a rush. 'How did it happen?'

'It just came to me, *Don't waste time trying anything else*. So I didn't.'

'What did you do?'

'I made the call and did what I was told. The women arranged everything, just as Sam said they would. I took a taxi to a corner of the railway station car park where there are always lots of people,' Gemma explained. 'At the exact time, a motorbike courier came up and took the package. It'll go by a messenger service to the prison where Jacob is and then to the librarian. She'll make sure he reads it as soon as possible. Any reply comes back the same way. No one else will touch it.'

She released a breath, imagining Jacob reading her note and then the play. 'I just hope he understands what I'm asking. Do you?'

'Kind of. But why didn't you go to the police. Can't those three be stopped?' Alice asked.

'From making threats? I think it's only when people do something that police can act. The supervision's supposed to keep those guys out of trouble.'

'It's not working?'

'They're even crazier since the fire,' Gemma swallowed. 'Without Jacob to impress, they're bored, he's their superhero now. How they get news of him I don't know?' She shuddered. 'I thought they were all talk, now I'm not sure. Not even sure about what I've just done.'

A long silence and then a faint sound. A sob? Poor Alice, not even safe in her own home. Gemma snapped out of her own darkening mood. 'Hey, I'm glad you texted. It's weird, us getting hassled at the same time.'

'What Sam suggested at the beach,' Alice whispered. 'Either tell Tracey, or get professional help, I should have done it.' Another gulp. 'I haven't changed at all, Gemma. I'm so scared.'

'Why wouldn't you be scared? Brad's bad news. And of course you've changed,' Gemma assured her. 'That was so smart, studying them like bugs. And your revenge spooked Dom and Carl brilliantly. Now you've got Brad on the run. What've you got left on him?'

Some nose blowing. 'Nothing. He's even quit smoking. I've probably improved his health.'

'There's something else, isn't there,' Gemma persisted.

More silence.

'Alice? Are you there?'

'It's Dad. Bloody hell, Gemma, Eric walked out on us, abandoned his own kids – ' More nose blowing. 'He's the cause of all this. I want to find him, if he's still alive.' Alice's voice, still small but determined. 'I want some answers from him. Maybe I'll use my wish too?'

Gemma gasped. 'Way to go, Alice! That'll test Sam's game, *whatever it is,*' she added.

'Maybe it's too long ago? Not even the right kind of danger?'

'Oh yes it is,' Gemma stared out her window, thinking fast. 'It's a great idea. Why not get something ready for when Sam calls back? Write down everything you can about your dad. It's Saturday, you can do it.'

She remembered Alice's story about the photos. 'You've still got those pictures of him? Get them ready too. Then you'll have the basics for finding him if Sam's thinks it's okay to ask.'

'Eric's bosses couldn't find him, and Mum's lawyers tried too' Alice answered. 'But I've got this feeling that Sam's friends might be different. Look at what they're doing for you.' Her voice sounded stronger. 'It's worth another try – at least I'll know if he's alive. And I hope Jacob sees sense and stops those three from stalking you. They sound like creeps.'

'They are. Hey, you've got your new clothes for when you meet Eric. It's fate, meant to be.' Keep her talking, Gemma decided.

'Not sure about that, but I'll put together a profile on him. It's a good idea.' Already Alice was speaking more easily.

'You've searched for him already, haven't you?'

'I've spent hours on the Internet, looking for his name in journals, conference reports, anywhere he might have published. I'll add that info as well, save anyone doing it again.'

Resourceful Alice back on track again, whew. 'Good thinking. I bet your brothers think about him too. If Brad gets nasty again, would telling him make him back off?'

'Not a chance. It's too risky, there's Tracey – she'd get the lawyers going and he'd – '

'Disappear again?' Gemma finished for her. 'Then we'll plan this together. No one else will know.'

'Plan what?'

'What to do. Suppose he is found, how will you get to see him without Tracey knowing? He could have gone to the Cayman Islands or something?'

Their conversation spun out of control then, reminding Gemma of their late night sessions in their room at the beach. After a while Alice said, 'I can't travel without Tracey finding out. But just getting some answers from him would be enough.'

Gemma heard new determination in her voice. 'If anyone can help, it'll be Sam,' she said. 'I'll let you get started.'

25

ALICE

Alice worked methodically behind her locked door, building up a profile of her father. Gemma had some wild notions but this one made sense.

Writing down Eric's physical description, age and personality, she frowned. He'd have altered, but how much? Tall, thin, narrow-shouldered, a shock of straight black hair and blue eyes from his Irish ancestry. Black hairs on the back of his long, narrow hands, should she put in little details like that?

Those hands had seemed huge to a child. She remembered them sorting his plant specimens, catalogue cards and photographs. Eric had been an obsessive collector and cataloguer. His joke that he'd saved the initial A for his daughter could even be true. Her brothers' initials were B, C and D, his own E. Alice shook her head. What kind of parent catalogued his own children?

She summarised what she'd already uncovered through public records; his education, university records, family details. Noted down sources of articles and papers he'd published during his teaching career.

Next she listed all she could find online about his last employer, a huge pharmaceutical company who'd recruited him to find medicinal plants in the Amazon rainforests of Brazil.

She wrote about seeing his hand-drawn maps and meticulous charts of plant families. Then notes abut his final photographs, those that she'd glimpsed anyway. Hollow-eyed, pot-bellied children with limbs like sticks. As a five year old, she'd wondered why they had no clothes.

Eric came across her staring at them and slammed the folder shut. Had she cried? She'd protested Alice knew, because he'd swept her up in a hug, promising to tell her about them one day. Held her close, told her how much he loved her. They were almost his last words to her.

Blinking back tears, Alice listed her own unsuccessful searches for any mention of his name. Surely she'd got enough?

Straightening up, she gathered the pages emerging from her printer, shuffled them together then impulsively added a few hand-written speculations of her own. *Impractical with money?* See Tracey's situation. *Not academically ambitious?* He'd never made Professor. With an insight into her own habits she noted, *Collects and catalogues to feel in control in a messy world?* Then she fitted everything into a folder.

A few hours later, Sam's long-awaited reply to her email arrived. 'Meet at your local cafe Royale 8 pm tonight?' She was here? What incredible luck. Noises from the TV room suggested an after-dinner sports game. Alice knew she wouldn't be missed.

She texted back and pulled the suitcase out from under the bed, choosing one of her new outfits to wear. Adding one of Gemma's tops, she covered it all with her raincoat. She arrived at the Royale a few minutes late to find Sam already there, resplendent in a Moroccan cape and harem trousers.

She cut off Alice's apology with a warm smile and wave of her hand. A tray of lemon tea for two arrived, Alice's favourite.

'Brad first,' Sam said, leaning forward and keeping her voice low. 'How safe are you? How serious is this threat of his? I know about your arm lock trick, but you won't catch him like that again.'

Trust Sam not to mess about with niceties. Alice silently thanked her for caring and for coming so far. She'd thought of little else but talking to her, even while writing about Eric.

'I don't think he'll physically hurt me,' she said, reddening. 'The threats were to frighten me and they worked.'

Sam touched her arm. 'Remember shame? Something's been hurt and needs to be mended?'

'Shame's a friend? Yes, I remember.' Alice gripped

her cup. 'Brad's no idea I've told anyone about – what happened with them. I think he's counted on me being too ashamed and scared. There'd be an uproar at home if Tracey found out. As the eldest he'd be held responsible and he won't risk that.' She leant forward, still speaking quietly. 'The problem is he's suspicious of me now. He's noticed I've changed, although not as much as I'd hoped. I can't imagine what he'll come up with next. I have to get away.'

'And you will. You're stronger now, Alice. You know it and Brad suspects it.' Sam reassured her. 'Of course he's on edge.'

She leaned back and loosened her cape and Alice took the chance to slip off her own coat, enjoying Sam's startled expression. 'You look lovely.'

Alice shared Gemma's scheme for using Jane's clothes charity and Sam shook her head. 'Did Jane know who the outfits were for?'

'Gemma said they were for a friend and used my situation. It's the first time I've worn any of them.' Alice smoothed the rose-coloured silk. 'Just knowing they're under the bed cheers me up. Gemma made this herself.'

'That girl, she'd never have made a lawyer. Sorry I didn't get back to you earlier, by the way. I've been travelling. Luckily my route brought me close enough to come here in person. I've wanted to see you. You've had a lot to deal with on your own, Alice.'

'I didn't expect you to come all this way, but I'm so glad you're here,' Alice slid her fingers lightly across her folder. 'I think I'll be okay around Brad for now, but I'd like your opinion on something else. It's a bit extreme but –'

'Tell me,' Sam sipped at her tea.

Alice explained the urge to find her father. 'Lately I even dream about him,' she gripped the folder. 'When I wake up, I'm furious. He should be here. None of this mess with Brad would have happened if he hadn't walked out.'

At Sam's raised eyebrows, she relented. 'Well, if he'd stayed, they'd have probably divorced. But he'd have been around. I need to find out if he's alive and get some answers.'

'If he is, would you expect him to come home?'

'If he's stayed away on purpose, no. It's too late.' Alice swallowed the lump in her throat. 'But I'd like to talk to him. That's why –' she slid the folder across to Sam. 'That's why I've done this. I want to use my emergency phone call for help to find him. Will this help me qualify, even though it's not a real crisis?'

Sam studied her for a long moment, then opened the folder and read. Alice leaned back as the pages were scanned, then shuffled together.

'This is excellent, Alice. Let's forget about Brad for now. If Eric's found, what do you want?'

'I want to talk to him,' Alice said. 'Face time, Skype,

I don't care.'

'Why now? After all these years?'

'It's hearing that Gemma used her wish,' Alice answered, noting Sam's start of surprise. So she didn't know? 'I'll let her tell you about it. So is my situation enough of an emergency?'

'It's unusual,' Sam admitted. 'It's partly a response to threats however.'

Alice let go a breath. 'Then I'll make the call?'

'Not so fast. Can I keep this?' Sam indicated the folder.

Alice nodded. 'I've kept a copy.'

'I've got some ideas. Let me see what the players can do,' Sam mused.

'But what about my wish? Is this it? Should I give the phone back to you?'

'Keep it for now. If Eric's found in some remote jungle and you have to travel to see him, there'll be danger enough for you.'

'But isn't that cheating? Having two calls?'

'Oh Alice,' Sam sighed. 'Let people help. You'd do the same, I know you would.'

'I can't travel anyway,' Alice shrugged. 'There's no way I could without Tracey knowing. What excuse could I give?'

'Maybe you're right. But let's be clear about a few things. Finding your father won't make Brad go away. You do know that, don't you?'

'It won't change Brad, but it might change me.'

'You're right. So, you want Eric found and to speak to him, if he's alive?'

Alice nodded.

'And if he's not?' Sam's voice held a warning note.

'At least I'll know.'

'There are many reasons people disappear, Alice. If he's in hiding, contact with you could come as a shock,' Sam persisted. 'He may have a new family. He may need your promise that you won't make any further demands. Can you give it?'

Alice swallowed. Could she? She agreed.

'I know it's hard, Alice but this is an unusual situation. Some compelling reason has stopped your father from getting in touch. A high-profile scientist is harder to lose than you might think.' She tapped her fingers on the pages. 'Your notes say the searches found no evidence of kidnappings of white people in the area? No news of a tall European amongst the tribes? Local people daren't conceal information like that, the retaliation is too great. His guides and staff all hunted for him. And his employers? Plus Tracey's lawyers?'

'He just disappeared,' Alice confirmed.

'You've written here that his employers paid his wages for six months after he was last seen and the household accounts were in joint names. So that's how Tracey managed?'

Alice nodded.

'And she hasn't wanted to marry again? Sell the house?'

Had she? Alice had never considered those parts of her mother's life. 'I don't think so.'

'Just as well,' Sam murmured. 'So much is impossible without a death certificate.'

'I didn't think of those things.' Cold fingers of doubt crept into Alice's mind.

Sam straightened the pages. 'A disappearance leaves a colossal mess for people to deal with, Alice. You find Tracey difficult but she's had her troubles too.'

Alice pushed away her tea, her hands trembling too much to pick up the cup.

'Do you still want to do this?' Sam's touch on her arm steadied her.

'I feel such a child, making a wish like a three-year old, as though I still believe in happy-ever-after endings.'

'You're intelligent and strong enough to hear what you're up against, Alice. That's why I'm telling you. I think it's a great idea and you've done all you can to help.' She held up the folder. 'This is more than the earlier investigations had, I'm sure.'

'The Fire Keeper accepts it then?'

'She does. No guarantees, you understand?'

'I understand.'

26

GEMMA

Just a few words, yet Gemma read them over and over, Jacob's sardonic voice echoing in her head.

'To Gemma, greetings. Your script reached me courtesy of the esteemed prison librarian. You have proved to be an attentive student, perhaps my only one. Your play embodies the ideals I spoke of but did not live. Will you? In anticipation of your future deeds, I will call off my dogs. J.'

Gemma clenched her fists but could not stop the tears squeezing out beneath her closed eyelids. She'd reached him. Her words had reached him. If she never wrote another thing, this would be enough. He believed in her!

'Who can I thank?' She telephoned Sam that evening to give her the news.

'I'll pass on your thanks, Gemma,' Sam agreed. 'And well done, for finishing your play. It must be compelling. Will you tell your parents about this?'

'Maybe, when the competition's over,' Gemma baulked at the suggestion. 'It'll be a relief not to see that car every day.'

'I'm sure. Gemma, thanks for the feedback but

I've people here, I need to go.'

'Oh, sorry.' Gemma phoned Alice next and told her the news. 'Now there's you,' she said after they'd talked it through. 'Heard anything about your dad?'

'Zilch.'

Gemma knew about waiting. 'What will you do if you hear they've found him?'

'Follow my instructions, I guess, like you did. Sam got me thinking about how hard it is for someone like him to disappear though. He must really not want to be found.'

'I suppose he's got his reasons. And Brad?'

'He's keeping his distance. And so am I.' They chatted some more. Then Alice cleared her throat. 'Gemma, you know this guy. Will he keep his word?'

'Jacob? Yes, I believe he will. Those words were a huge concession from a person like him.'

'Your play must be good.'

'Maybe.'

27

ALICE

Sam phoned some weeks later, on a Thursday evening. With Tracey working late and her brothers watching TV, Alice was in her room and could talk undisturbed.

'Alice, I've only got a moment,' Sam's shrill tone made her sound eerily like Tracey. Alice frowned at the phone, was she ill?

'Your friend's alive and well,' Sam went on gaily.

Alice sank onto her bed, deciphering the words and Sam's strange manner. Eric? It must be.

'He's willing to talk to you, but there are conditions and we'll help you meet them,' Sam twittered. Someone must be listening, someone Sam didn't trust.

Alice clutched at the phone, joy exploding in her chest. She needed to hear it again. 'Someone's talked to *him*?'

'There's been some communication.'

'Where – where is he?'

Sam's voice rose theatrically. 'That I don't *know*! Alice, it's going to take *ever* such a long time to set this up, can we talk about it another day?' That sugary tone could only signal caution?

'And let's keep it a sweet little surprise, just between us?' Sam added. 'Promise?'

'No problem!' Alice matched Sam's absurd voice to show she understood. 'Thanks for the *lovely* news, hear from you later.'

Putting down the phone, she punched at her pillows, clenching her lips to keep from screaming. Her father, alive and he wanted to talk to her. Not a sweet little surprise, a miracle. Somehow those amazing women had pulled it off.'

She replayed the strange conversation. Sam avoiding Eric's name. Her coded instruction to say nothing. What had her absent father done? He couldn't just be avoiding Tracey. But Sam's instructions were clear. Alice mustn't talk about it, even to Gemma.

28

GEMMA

Gemma stared at her cousin. 'Sam wrote you a *letter?*'

'Yup, one of those things we sent to our grandparents when they were alive, remember? Thank you for the book, I liked it.' Alice chuckled.

'Sam wrote to thank you for something? I don't get it.'

'Sam wrote to me because 'Phone calls, emails and text messages are not the best option for secure communication.' ' Alice sketched quotation marks in the air with her fingers. 'Because – ' she dropped her voice although they were alone, 'they've found Eric.'

Gemma's head jerked up. 'He's alive? Where? Have you talked to him?'

'I wasn't allowed to phone or text you about it. Or email.' Alice flung herself onto the bed and poured out her news, beginning with Sam's strange phone call.

They were in Gemma's room, even though they had the whole house to themselves. Alice was staying over for the weekend while Jane and Henry were at a conference.

What with Alice behaving oddly, refusing to talk

about anything but school, clothes and ordinary things, they hadn't caught up properly in a while. But listening to her now raving on about vetted software and robust operating systems, Gemma could scarcely keep up with her.

'So Eric's alive?' she broke in. 'Somewhere in Brazil, and in hiding? And he won't talk to anyone but you and only through an iPod Touch? Is he serious? IPod's are history – '

'They may be history to you but it so happens I've still got one. It was a combined birthday and Christmas present from everyone and I'm very proud of it.' Alice pretended to pout. 'I've posted it to Sam so she can get an encrypted voice communications app. installed and other weird stuff done to it. That means I can talk to Dad and there'll be no traces. An iPod Touch isn't linked to any phone systems, so they can be made secure. Journalists use them, maybe even spies.'

'Why the secrecy? What's he done?' Gemma put on her lucky hat. She needed help to follow all this. 'And what's with the letter?'

'That's how Sam explained everything to me, in her letter. Eric's situation is so dangerous she's been asked not to mention his name on any telecommunications device. I'm not too keen on using them myself, since I learned how much they're monitored.'

'I thought you were upset about something, when you wouldn't talk.'

'Then you were wrong. And Sam hasn't been able to meet me since that cafe visit I told you about, so that's why she wrote. This goes no further than us, Gemma.'

'I know. It won't. I promise. So what's it like, knowing you'll get to talk to your dad?' Gemma had to ask.

'Like a thick fog's lifted off my brain. Like I'm seeing and hearing clearly for the first time in years.'

'You? The smart kid? The scientist?'

'It's different,' Alice gazed at the ceiling. 'I didn't know the fog was there. It's like a door's opened and fresh air's rushed in. And light. There were a lot of dark memories I didn't want to look at. Now I'm not so scared.'

'Sounds great to me,' Gemma got up. 'Let's get some food, you can tell me more while we cook.'

'Do you ever think of that first day at Sam's?' Alice asked later, stirring a sauce in the kitchen. 'How edgy we were around each other?'

'And around Sam,' Gemma added. 'Then Aishe. Remember Ingrid with her motorbike?'

'And Denise,' Alice laughed. 'I hope she recovered from me falling apart and trying to kill her.'

'Just as well you did, fall apart I mean. We were both tied up in knots. I was a train wreck, badly in need of Sam's game.' She grinned at Alice. '*Whatever it is*. Whatever it is, it started with kindness. Then confidence.'

'Don't forget cooperation,' Alice added. 'Sam said it was a normal way to live once. When? And where?'

Gemma loaded their plates and they sat down to eat. 'Any clues about what's happened to your dad? Don't tell me if you don't want to.'

'I've got a feeling it's to do with some kids,' Alice said. 'He had photos of them. They were the one thing in my notes on him that was different. Everything else was about plants.' She described the children as she remembered them, big-eyed, pot-bellied, limbs like sticks and strangely beautiful. Gemma could imagine their impact on a little girl.

'Sam wrote that when he was still working with Amazon tribes, his Portuguese nickname was Pai pequeno. It means little father,' Alice hesitated. 'I think it's a joke.'

'I don't get it.' Gemma didn't understand.

'In his last job he was helped by the Awa people. They're quite small, some people call them pygmies but I don't. Being small works in the rainforests, you can move around easily and it's better for hunting. Lots of other species are smaller in rainforests too, I've read about it.'

'Okay, okay, he's tall, they're small and maybe they gave him the name for a joke. But –?'

'Why father? It doesn't have to mean he's got kids there. Awa men share the children, it's called plural paternity.' She shifted uncomfortably. 'I was glad to read that myself. My guess is they called him that because he helped with the kids maybe? Perhaps with medicine?'

'Wouldn't all Westerners going to places like that take medicine?' Gemma caught Alice's look. 'Sorry, I'm pouring cold water on your idea.'

'You're right, it's just a feeling I've got.' Alice pushed away her plate. 'But why go into hiding? I hope he hasn't done anything too awful.'

'Does Sam know how he was found?'

'If she does, she's giving nothing away. Our mysterious women's network has to be kept safe. We're so lucky, Gemma. Just think if we'd been born in the Amazon, bulldozers could be smashing down our homes. Over a hundred thousand kilometres of Amazon rainforest get wrecked every year.' She jumped up and took her plate to the bench. 'D'you know what I'd like to do after we've finished here? I'd like to read your play.'

Gemma looked up. 'Really? Then you're in luck. I've just printed off another copy. Sam said they'd have shredded mine at the prison. Can I read your notes on Eric?'

Gemma finished long before Alice. Watching her cousin stretched out on the sofa, still absorbed in the play, Gemma tried to read her expression. Did she like it? Better still, did she get it? Another page turned and

Gemma held her breath.

Alice frowned then flicked back a page. Gemma leapt to her feet, she couldn't stand it any longer. She'd go online and look at the area where Eric had last been seen. But after only a few clicks, she'd couldn't take any more of that either. Loggers, squatters and fabulously rich cattle ranchers, all encroaching on the Amazon rainforest with their bulldozers and chain saws. Millions of people reduced to living in mud huts once the forest was gone, no home, no job, no land, no opportunities. Most of them still under twenty-five, and all apprehensive about the future.

Eric's work had been finding medicinal plants to exploit before they disappeared under the bulldozers. He'd be about as popular as a convoy of earthmoving machines. Poor Alice.

29

ALICE

Alice appreciated Gemma's play and said so. It wasn't only the characters and their story. Even she could follow Gemma's stage directions and visualise what she wanted to happen. But what about the seeds of the plot, where did they come from?

Gemma was vague. 'I don't know, out of the air? But I do my research after the ideas come, just like you do.' She tapped Alice's folder.

'Your title, 'More dangerous than a thousand rioters'? Who is this Lucy Parsons?' Alice asked.

'Someone remembered as a 'powerful and perilous speaker'. That's why the papers gave her that by-line.' Gemma counted on her fingers. 'Female, coloured, a child of slaves, radical supporter of the poor, in a mixed marriage. Who'd expect a woman like that to have any impact in 1920's US?'

Alice handed the folder back. 'If you keep on writing like this, you're going to need a bodyguard.'

They talked about Gemma's plans, about Eric, Alice's own future, about Sam and Sam's-game-whatever-it-is, and more. Alice also helped Gemma sort all her playwriting paraphernalia.

'There's so much to learn,' Gemma groaned. 'Even to write a play. I have to know about different kinds of theatres. Then staging, characterization, plots, dialogue. Plus roles like producers and directors and what they do. I've been downloading everything I find. What with my sketchbooks and stuff for school, I can't find a thing any more.'

Alice considered the chaotic heaps of books and papers. 'I need a project to get my mind off Eric and you need a filing system. Let's go to the shops.'

While Gemma shopped for fresh food, Alice loaded a trolley in the nearby stationery store. Talk about role reversals. She remembered Gemma on her first day in Sam's kitchen and smiled.

It didn't take them long to sort the papers in Gemma's room into piles. 'This will save my life – and my grades,' Gemma pranced around the towers of neatly labelled colour-coded boxes. 'You've got more from your cataloguing dad than your blue eyes,' she added. 'And he was Irish? I didn't know that. Maybe I'll research my parents too.'

Do it soon, before it's too late. Alice didn't say the words aloud. 'What shall we do now?' she asked instead.

'Why not write down your main questions for your dad?' Gemma suggested. 'Sam said you won't have long to talk.'

'If I could only see his face,' Alice crushed an old envelope between her hands. 'Suppose I don't even recognise his voice?'

Wordlessly, Gemma handed her a pen and paper.

Sam's coded instructions should have prepared her, but Eric's voice when Alice heard it a week later was so familiar that her knees gave way and she had to sit down on her bed. She was a child again with her beloved father beside her.

Except that he wasn't. It was years later, she was seventeen years old, in her room alone – and she had questions to ask, hard questions.

But so did he, and hers could wait. Alice rapidly updated him on the family situation, health, study, occupations and such, including her plans for a botany scholarship – heavy emphasis on *scholarship.* I've got no study fund, she wanted to scream but didn't. When she'd finished, Eric fell silent.

'Why?' Alice asked her first question. 'Why did you leave? Was it the children?'

A sharp intake of breath. 'You remember those photos?'

'Of course I do. And your reaction to me seeing them.'

'You were so young.' He cleared his throat noisily. 'But you were smart.'

'Why?' Alice persisted.

'Alice, we may never speak again. You know that?'

'I know.' Alice pulled her notes and pen closer.

'I'll tell you, but you tell no one else, for your own safety, for mine and thousands of others. Okay?'

She heard him gulp in air. 'I promise,' she said.

'I've done bad things, Alice. You're well rid of me. You know what's happening here in the Amazon? The deforestation making millions homeless? Wrecking the land, fouling the water?' He heaved a sigh at her reply. 'Well, I've helped bomb railroads, blow up bridges, destroy logging roads, possibly killed people even while I was working here as a scientist. Before you saw me for the last time, Alice.'

It was her turn to gasp.

'So now you know the worst. And you're right, it was the children. They helped do these things as well, and I couldn't bear the hardness growing in them. So I backed off to figure out a better way to help save the Amazon. Then someone said to me, 'Start from where you are.' So, no more bombing, Alice, no more wrecking things. Now I grow trees.'

'You what?' Alice cried. Was he mad?

'Rainforest takes years to grow so I use plant tissue culture, not cuttings or seeds. It speeds up the process immeasurably. I'm actually quite good at it. Selecting the best trees, the best plants to use. My lab is hidden but a few special people know where to find me. My main helpers I never meet, the old people, mothers, children, men injured from the fighting.

A guerilla army planting trees.'

Alice gulped. 'Then why the secrecy? Isn't planting trees good?'

'I'm a wanted man, Alice,' Eric sounded completely calm. 'After everything else I'd done, I stole to set this up. I needed a lot of equipment. A gas powered sterilization unit, a humidity tent. Tools, Agar, plant nutrients, building supplies. Others helped but it took time. And then I disappeared.'

Her curiosity roused, Alice asked, 'How many?'

'How many trees? More than thirty million so far, Alice. Those wretched forest fires spread into areas too remote for cattle or soy and cash crops. That becomes our land, inaccessible and far from roads.' He chuckled. 'How many people? Thousands. It's labour intensive work. My friends even train teams of small children. Their little fingers are ideal for cleaning nutrients off the new roots and settling the plantlets into outdoor beds to harden off.' He paused. 'Are you with me so far?'

'Go on,' Alice imagined the scene.

'Everyone helps once the plants are big enough to go in the ground and they care for the trees after that. Tribes travel a lot, it works well.' His tone lightened. 'You can add child labour to my crimes but the little ones love it. They learn new skills and try out the botanical names, just like you did.'

How could he joke about something like this? Alice

choked back a sob.

'Oh Alice, don't think I haven't thought about you all,' her father burst out. 'I've agonised over what I did. But I was lost to marriage years ago. Tracey and I fell apart after Brad was born, and my trips away made it worse. We kept trying to make it work and then crashing. I'd be so happy to see you kids healthy and smart, and then I'd ache for the kids here. I was making their lives even worse. I couldn't stay and I couldn't go.'

'And now you can stay.' It wasn't a question.

'Yes, and I'll go on doing this as long as I'm able. The people plant food as well, we look after each other.'

Alice pushed her list of questions away. How could she complain about her own life after this?

'And you, Alice?' Her father pressed on. 'You found me, after everyone else failed. Little Alice, grown up and able to pull off something like this? I'm honoured to spend this time with you.'

He wasn't laughing at her. If only she could see his face. 'I've been lucky,' she said. 'I've met women who care about me too.'

'Two women told me what you wanted; I was stunned. At first I wouldn't risk it, but they persuaded me to trust you. I'm sorry, Alice, but you know what's at stake.'

A long pause. Had he finished?

'They claimed to be part of what must be a very long

chain. I don't want to know how it works but I'm glad you've got women you can trust. And that you trust yourself, Alice. I'm so happy for you.'

'I've had help,' she said again. 'Heaps of it. I've missed you and been mad at you, Dad but I'm proud of you now. I'm glad you're okay and I'm okay too.' Tears spilled over, warm and soft. Snuffling noises came from him too.

'Hey Alice, that's the best thing anyone could hear, thank you.' Alice heard nose blowing. 'So, botany studies for you, eh? You might talk to these people.' He rattled off a few names and she scribbled them down. Then it was time to go.

When the connection ended, Alice fell back onto her bed and lay there. What risks he'd taken and what a cost. Yet he sounded buoyant, full of fun. He loved his life. Crazy man!

Clutching her notes to her, Alice replayed every word in her mind. The fullness in her chest left no room for doubts. What a wonder, talking to him and feeling such connection. They might never speak again yet she knew him as well as she was beginning to know herself. It was enough.

30

GEMMA

Although her curiosity ran wild, Gemma accepted that Alice couldn't tell her much about Eric except that he was alive, in good spirits and doing work to help the rainforest. He'd seriously annoyed a few people in the process so he couldn't come home. And he and Alice had no plans to speak again. That was all.

Gemma agreed to never speak of it again, even between themselves. There'd been much more, she knew. Alice was a changed person since that conversation, no longer bitter about her brothers and Tracey, and keen to try new things, take more risks.

Alice regularly urged Gemma to join her on her new adventures. So they'd volunteered for tree planting on an island bird sanctuary and for the first time in their lives, run shrieking down a mountainside in a howling gale, arms outstretched and hair flying. They'd joined a late night soup run serving food to the homeless, where Gemma filled a notebook with sketches and snatches of conversation so bizarre she could never have invented it.

Alice also had her sights set on a Science Made

Simple competition with rules stipulating that entries must fit a tight budget. She'd called her entry Guerilla Gardening with Bombs and laughed idiotically every time she mentioned it.

Gemma read her latest email asking for feedback and studied the attached plans and illustrations. The words Guerilla Gardener decorated an old backpack. Inside were Alice's Gardening for Free Guidelines describing how to save seeds and take cuttings from un-pruned public parks and gardens. Photos showed guerilla gardeners planting roadside verges and gave contact details of groups to join. Gemma liked the bright colours of her two homemade plant hangers made from recycled materials, one to drape over walls, the other to wrap around parking meters and lamp posts. There was also a vegetable seed kit with ideas on how to garden in vacant land, plus secateurs, a gardening fork and trowel. Finally a cardboard egg carton holding six seed bombs with instructions for making more. The whole lot fitted into the pack and cost well within the budget limit.

Scientific or not it looked simple enough, but what was a seed bomb? Gemma read the recipe. It turned out to be nothing more than garden clay and compost mixed with a little water to make small balls with seeds inside. Parsley and coriander, poppies and marigolds were suitable apparently. Once dried, the bombs could be chucked into bare woodlands, onto beachfronts and riverbanks, any vacant land where they might grow. If the guerilla gardener could walk by to water and weed them that would be a bonus. Gemma made a few suggestions and emailed it back. She'd her own project to work on.

Gemma wanted drama studies taught across all streams in their school. She'd talked to several teachers but only one would hear her out.

'You're leaving here soon, Gemma,' the woman protested, after listening to her. 'Why the fuss?'

'Acting's our most fundamental way of learning,' Gemma had her arguments ready. 'Kinesthetic learning through action. It's a crime to take it out of general education.'

'But our curriculum, it's already so full.'

'That's because it takes too long to teach some subjects. Not everyone learns from books. Acting out events speeds up comprehension, impacts on long-term memory.'

'You're very sure of yourself. How do you know all this?'

'I've seen it work, at a – summer school.' Gemma improvised.

'Then write me a proposal by the end of next week and I'll consider it. And thank you Gemma, for thinking of younger girls.'

Girls as bored as I was, Gemma muttered as she left.

Above her desk at home, beside the programme from their original play, she'd pinned a recent letter. Although her competition entry hadn't been placed, the judges' letter gave such encouraging feedback that even Jane took notice. Gemma knew she'd been crazy to attempt it, knowing so little about acting. Other girls at her school deserved a better start.

Attraction, she wrote. *Creativity. Active involvement.* Her fingers flew over the computer keys.

31

ALICE

Alice re-read the invitation on her phone, sinking onto a chair in surprise. 'The Fire Keeper invites you to meet new players, certain you'll have much useful support to offer.' The date and details followed. She and Gemma were to visit Sam's for a few hours only but wouldn't be able to stay over.'

Closing her eyes, Alice saw the beach again, her bedroom window with its view of the stars, and Sam. Nothing would stop her from going, from contributing in any way that she could. It would be tacit thanks for stuff she could never speak of again, and for her chance at a new beginning.

In a long letter to Sam, Alice had tried to express her gratitude for release from the fog of self-loathing she'd generated since childhood. She now knew that many small children blame themselves when parents leave. She also had her own private gratitude that Pai pequeno could forgive himself too and focus on his new offspring, growing in their millions in his remote nurseries.

At Sam's, she and Gemma would meet new players in the Game. Was it going well for them, whoever they were? While most girls thrived, there were a few not able to move on. Some fell back into unhealthy situations because they felt familiar; others gave up. 'It's not the right time for them,' Sam said, when Alice asked her about it. 'And it's not our business.' Eric had been advised to start from where he was and he had. It's all anyone can do, even if it means starting over and over again.

Alice hadn't won anything at the Science show but she'd had fun and met new people. Many invitations to join guerilla gardening groups came her way, but it wasn't her time for them either.

She'd contacted the people Eric mentioned and been asked to send in her details. Three scholarship applications were already on their way, helped by top marks, references from two teachers and one from a player, an agricultural scientist who'd questioned her closely during several Skype interviews. Who knew where she'd study, but whatever happened she was no longer alone.

Her phone rang. Gemma, of course. 'Shall we drive down to Sam's together? Henry's letting me take his car.' No preliminaries, just like Sam. They chatted for ages, speculating on who might be at the beach, who they might meet.

'Is Tracey getting used to you going away to uni next year?' Gemma asked.

'Tracey's so busy planning Brad and Justine's future, I could join the space race and she wouldn't notice,' Alice snorted then added, 'No, that's not fair. Tracey's fine, she enjoyed her time at the Science show and kept telling everyone I was her daughter. All her clients know about my backpacks and the salon's even running a raffle to sponsor some.'

'The photos were great, you posing in your designer clothes! Some guerilla gardener you'd be. Don't you dare wear them while you're making seed bombs.'

'I'll wear one of your tops to Sam's though, I might get you some new orders?' Alice teased.

'Whatever,' Gemma's voice fell.

'What's wrong?'

'Jane and Henry are arguing a lot lately. If I hadn't pushed him, Henry might be still doing law and not playing around with old houses. I should have left him alone.'

'Your mother doesn't like change, does she?'

'She still thinks theatre's a passing phase for me. That I'll get a real job once I've found out here's no money in it.'

'And Henry?'

'He's thrilled that I like what I do. He's changed so much. He used to go along with Jane all the time, now he just looks her in the eye and says his piece.'

'Is he happier?' Alice asked.

'Hard to say, but he's a lot more alive.' Gemma's voice lifted. 'There's no happily-ever-after anyway. We all die.'

'Oh, thanks for nothing. Been reading your existentialists again?'

Gemma laughed. 'A few people got worried when I started quoting Simone de Beauvoir at school. The librarian said her book is always on loan, for the sex bits probably. No, I don't read much these days, what with making costumes and working backstage every minute that I'm not studying.'

'And loving it. You've fallen on your feet with that theatre group. I didn't know acrobatics, art and acting could be mixed up together into one show.'

'That's why they need so many volunteers,' Gemma laughed.

'Lucky for you. Learning any more new words?'

Here's one for you,' Gemma offered. 'Stage rake. Three guesses.'

'A sleazy actor? A tool for tidying up after a messy show? I give up.'

'The slope of a stage up from the audience,' Gemma told her.

'Something to drop into a conversation, I suppose. How's your stage rake?'

They made plans to meet and to send their acceptances to Sam. 'Are you nervous about being one of the newest Fire Keeper's girls?' Gemma asked. 'Suppose someone asks us what the game's about?'

'A bit,' Alice answered. 'But I doubt anyone will ask us anything like that. I can only say how it's been for me anyway. What about you?'

'I'm excited and scared at the same time. So much has happened since we were there last. If anyone asks about Sam's-Game-whatever-it-is? I'd say, find out what you do to hold yourself back from being happy. After you face up to that, no one can manipulate you again. And you won't ever need to blame others.'

'Then I'd say, the best of yourself is totally worth claiming. Give it everything you've got to find it – and enjoy it.'

'That's what we found anyway,' Gemma said. 'Gemma and Alice, the Fire Keeper's girls.'

The Women

Alicia Alonso (1921–) *Cuba*	**Te Puea Herangi** (1883–1952) *New Zealand*
Simone de Beauvoir (1908–1986) *France*	**Emily Hobhouse** (1860–1926) *UK*
Aphra Behn (1640–1689) *England*	**Dolores Huerta** (1930–) *Mexican-US*
Hildegard of Bingen (1098–1179) *Germany*	**Sofia Kovalevskaya** (1850–1891) *Russia*
Berta Cáceres (1972–2016) *Honduras*	**Wangari Maathai** (1940–2011) *Kenya*
Helen Caldicott (1938–) *Australia*	**Lise Meitner** (1878–1968) *Austria*
Rachel Carson (1907–1964) *US*	**He Ming Qing** aka **Kathleen Hall** (1896-1970) *China/New Zealand*
Alexandra David-Néel (1868–1969) *Belgium*	**Wilma Rudolph** (1940–1994) *US*
Chökyi Drönma (1422–1456) *Tibet*	**Sophia Scholl** (1921–1943) *Germany*
Shirin Ebadi (1947–) *Iran*	**Irena Sendler** (1910–2008) *Poland*
Marie-Louise von Franz (1915–1998) *Switzerland*	**Helen Sharman** (1963–) *UK*
Margaret Heafield Hamilton (1936–) *US*	**Mitsu Tanaka** (1945–) *Japan*
	Early Women in Medicine *Egypt, Greece, Italy, Germany, Scotland, Sweden and more.*

Alicia Alonso (1921–)

How does a young mother with only partial sight in one eye and no peripheral vision dance as guest star in Giselle with ballet companies ranging from the Paris Opéra Ballet to the Royal Danish Ballet, and become the first dancer from the West to perform in the Soviet Union?

Cuban-born Alicia brought extraordinary passion and determination to every area of her life. A dancer from an early age, at 16 she impulsively married fellow ballet student Fernando Alonso and moved to New York City where their daughter Laura was born. Alicia continued training at the School of American Ballet and took private classes when she could.

At 21, Alicia was operated on for a detached retina and had to lie blinded by bandages and motionless in bed for three months so her eyes could heal. Unable to resist, she pointed and stretched her feet, '*just to keep them alive*' she said. Perhaps due to this, the surgery proved unsuccessful, as did a second operation and Alicia eventually agreed to a third in Havana.

Following this procedure, she had to lie motionless in bed for an entire year. She could not engage with little Laura, laugh, cry or even chew food too hard.

Her husband sat with her every day, moving her fingers to teach her the great dancing roles of classical ballet. She recalled during that period, *'I danced in my mind. Blinded, motionless, flat on my back, I taught myself to dance Giselle.'*

Finally able to leave her bed, once she'd recovered her strength Alicia returned to New York. They'd barely arrived when Alicia danced Giselle for the Ballet Theatre, replacing their injured prima ballerina. Her outstanding performance led to Alicia becoming their new prima ballerina within three years, regardless of her ongoing vision problems.

Alicia was celebrated as an intensely dramatic dancer, an awe-inspiring and skilled interpreter of both classical and romantic repertoires. She guided her male ballet partners into such flawless partnerships that they would move to exactly where she needed them. Set designers installed strong spotlights in different colors to guide her movements and stretched a thin invisible wire across the edge of the stage at waist height.

Alicia and Fernando determined to bring ballet to Cuba as well and before she turned 30, they founded the Alicia Alonso Ballet Company in Havana with Fernando as general director and his choreographer brother Alberto as artistic director. As well as teaching, Alicia continued her career as a sought-after prima ballerina, dancing in Russia and Paris and commuting to the US. When American audiences rejected her after the 1962 ballistic missile crisis, Alicia continued to perform in Canada where reviewers hailed her as 'still the greatest ballerina of her time.' Alicia danced solos in Europe and elsewhere well into her 70's. A 2015 documentary film *Horizontes* features her life story.

Simone de Beauvoir (1908–1986)

Throughout her life and in all her writing, Simone challenged the cultural assumption that women's very nature and role and function in society is innately inferior to men's.

Her best-known book, *The Second Sex* (1949) outlines the global extent of women's widespread oppression throughout history, as a result of being categorized as the *other*. Simone explains this categorization after observing that in society, the male is seen as representing the *self,* the essential and the female as the *other,* the inessential. To support her argument, along with her other research Simone explored mythology. In ancient creation myths, many of which have found their way into the three linked religions, Judaism, Christianity and Islam, she found women labelled as the unknown, dark and mysterious that attracts men even while they fear it. Subsequent religious sanctions allowing men to both scapegoat and disparage women has confirmed their persistent illusion of superiority.

Simone writes that women's struggle in liberating themselves economically, politically, and sexually from the role of *other* is a difficult undertaking, given this ideological mistrust. She nevertheless insists that part of this reversal requires women to acknowledge and enjoy the biological differences between men and women.

The Second Sex, a 972-page study, inspired women worldwide while many male-dominated establishments condemned it. Unfortunately, Simone's revolutionary research wasn't fully appreciated amongst non-French speaking readers until the tentative 1953 English version was finally replaced with a more accurate translation in 2009.

At age 21, Simone formed a life-long, sexual relationship with fellow writer Jean-Paul Sartre but refused to marry him or live in the same house with him. She felt that in the prevailing European culture, this would cramp both their lives and their writing. The works of both these great French authors reflect existentialist ideas (see below) and each had a great regard for the other's abilities, refusing to publish before consulting each other. Simone published many more non-fiction and fiction books and died six years after her best friend. They lie together in Paris in the same grave.

Existentialism: 19th century Danish thinker, Søren Kierkegaard, proposed to modern European society that each individual—and not society or religion—is solely responsible for giving meaning to life and living it passionately and sincerely, or 'authentically.' This challenge to dominant external authorities was later termed Existentialism. In Existential thought, both freedom and authenticity are seen as supreme values and the systematic or academic philosophies are considered too remote from actual human experience.

Aphra Behn (1640–1689)

Aphra is the first Englishwoman known to have supported herself financially as an author, and also the first prolific and high profile female dramatist.

During the 1670s and 1680s, Aphra's published output as an English writer was second only to Poet Laureate, John Dryden. She is quoted as saying she had *'led a life dedicated to pleasure and poetry.'*

After the death of her husband only two years into a childless marriage, Aphra worked as a political spy in Antwerp for King Charles 11 during the second Anglo-Dutch war. Unpaid for her services and impoverished on her return to London, she turned to writing in order to survive and began to publish satirical comments about the political and social events of the court.

Following the defeat of Puritan rule in England and the return from Holland of the exiled Charles 11, the restored royal court became notorious for its lavish, sometimes scandalous entertainments. By then an esteemed poet, novelist, playwright, short story writer and feminist, Aphra published and had performed under Royal patronage at least nineteen bawdy and comic plays celebrated for their wit and humour.

Her lengthy poem, 'The Disappointment'* about an attempted rape of a virginal girl and the humiliating impotence of the would-be rapist, displays her astute observation and writing skill.

At Court and in society, Aphra was celebrated for engaging in vigorous written debates with contemporary male writers, defending the ability of women to engage in intellectual pursuits. Regrettably no records have been found showing other women of her time benefitting from and being encouraged by her example.

Aphra continued to write on a wide range of topics even as her health failed, although it became increasingly hard for her to hold a pen. In the final days of her short life, she finished her translation of the final book of Abraham Cowley's *Six Books of Plants,* completing her work on the series.

She is buried in Westminster Abbey amongst other mostly male writers and artists.

*Extract from 'The Disappointment'

He Curst his Birth, his Fate, his Stars,
But more the Shepherdesses Charms;
Whose soft bewitching influence,
Had Damn'd him to the Hell of Impotence.

Hildegard of Bingen (1098–1179)

Hildegard supervised the miniature illuminations in the Rupertsberg manuscript of her first work, Scivias (Know the Ways). This miniature shows her dictating what she sees in a vision to her male scribe and secretary.

The tenth child of a German Countess, at eight years old Hildegard was made a servitor to an anchoress (a religious woman living in solitude) and at fourteen entered a Benedictine monastery enclosing both men and women, where her aunt was abbess. At age thirty-eight, Hildegard was appointed abbess and remained in this role until her eighties.

All her life, Hildegard energetically rebelled against dispiriting religious, cultural and social restrictions in Germany. She undertook four extensive preaching tours to deliver apocalyptic sermons on widespread corruption among the clergy. At 81 in the last year of her life, she successfully opposed a church edict and narrowly escaped being turned out of her convent with her nuns by a horde of outraged priests.

Along with her leaflets and sermons, Hildegard wrote nine books ranging across cosmology, botany, linguistics, theology and medical science,

In her medical texts, she described circulation of the blood, the connection between sugar and diabetes, the relationship of the brain to the nervous system and more, anticipating numerous scientific 'discoveries' by several centuries. Hildegard is also credited with writing the first clear description of the female orgasm. She is considered to be the founder of scientific natural history in Germany, where Naturopathic doctors still practice 'Hildegard Medizin' and work with her dietary philosophy. She also composed several hundred songs, some of which are still performed today.

Since childhood, Hildegard was known for her ecstatic visions that brought her such joy and inspired much of her research and writing. She was in her early forties when church officials endorsed her as 'A genuine recipient of Revelation.' Following one vision, she wrote:

> *'I, the fiery life of divine essence, am aflame beyond the beauty of the meadows. I gleam in the waters. I burn in the sun, moon, and stars. With every breeze, as with invisible life that contains everything, I awaken everything to life. I am the breeze that nurtures all things green. I encourage blossoms to flourish with ripening fruits. I am the rain coming from the dew that causes the grasses to laugh with the joy of life.'*

Berta Cáceres (1972–2016)

Berta was a Honduran environmental activist, indigenous leader and co-founder and coordinator of the Council of Popular and Indigenous Organizations of Honduras (COPINH). She won the Goldman Environmental Prize in 2015 for successfully pressuring the world's largest dam builder to pull out of building the Agua Zarca Dam on indigenous people's land at the Gualcarque River.

Born into the Lenca people in La Esperanza, southwestern Honduras, Berta grew up in troubled times in Central America. Her mother Austra, a midwife and social activist, was also an elected mayor, congresswoman and area governor and took in refugees from El Salvador. Berta studied to be a teacher. She also led many COPINH protest campaigns on issues including illegal logging and the presence of US military bases on Lenca land, supported feminism, LGBT rights and indigenous people's rights.

In 2006, indigenous Lenca people from Río Blanco asked Berta to investigate construction equipment arriving in their area. She uncovered a joint venture project between the Chinese company Sinohydro, the World Bank's International Finance Corporation, and a Honduran company Desarrollos Energéticos, S.A. (also known as DESA). They planned to construct four hydroelectric dams on the Gualcarque River.

The developers had breached international law by failing to consult with the local people on the project that would compromise the Lenca people's access to water, food and materials for medicine, and threaten their traditional way of life. Berta worked with the community on a protest campaign and took the case to the Inter-American Commission on Human Rights. A 2009 military coup left Honduras open to even more environmental exploitation after a sell-off of mining and hydroelectric concessions.

From 2013, Berta led a COPINH and local community protest at the Gualcarque River construction site. Military and security officers harassed and removed protesters and on 15 July 2013 opened fire, killing one member of COPINH and injuring three others. Two later attacks left two more protesters dead and three seriously injured.

COPINH's protests led both Sinohydro and the International Finance Corporation to withdraw from the project. DESA then moved the construction site and officials filed criminal charges against Berta and others for their roles in the protest. Dozens of regional and international organizations, including Amnesty

International, petitioned the Honduran government to stop criminalizing defenders of human rights.

On 20 February 2016, more than 100 protesters were arrested and threats increased. On 2 March 2016 Berta was shot dead in her home by armed intruders. Her four children survived. Some of those arrested for her murder were in special forces units of the Honduran military trained at Fort Benning, Georgia, US. Berta had been on their hit list for months.

In November 2017, a team of international legal experts found '*willful negligence*' by US, Dutch and Finnish financial institutions who worked with DESA and Honduras state security agencies '*to control, neutralize and eliminate any opposition*' to the dam. Berta had been right all along. She said, '*I want to live, but I have never once considered giving up fighting for our territory, for a life with dignity, because our fight is legitimate.*'

Helen Caldicott (1938–)

A 2004 documentary film, *Helen's War: Portrait of a Dissident*, looks into Helen's life as a long-term activist against nuclear energy through the eyes of her niece, filmmaker Anna Broinowski. For much of her life Helen has led an international campaign to educate the public about the medical hazards of the nuclear age, and the changes needed in human behavior to stop such environmental destruction.

She trained as a pediatrician in Adelaide, Australia just as the impact of nuclear radiation on unborn and young children was becoming more widely known and in the 1970s, she and her husband campaigned publicly on its health hazards. She helped to convince Australia and New Zealand into protesting against the testing of nuclear weapons in the Pacific, and has given influential lecture tours in New Zealand.

Following the 1979 Three Mile Island nuclear accident in Pennsylvania, Helen left her medical career to concentrate on calling world attention to the nuclear arms race and the growing reliance on nuclear power. She founded women's groups in the US and elsewhere, dedicated to moving government spending away from nuclear energy into meeting social issues, and to educating people about the medical dangers of nuclear energy, nuclear weapons and nuclear war.

Helen has written and edited many books. While touring with her sixth book, *The New Nuclear Danger (2001)*, she founded an influential organisation with its headquarters in Washington D.C. now known as *Beyond Nuclear: Working for a world free from nuclear power and nuclear weapons.* In 2008 she founded the Helen Caldicott Foundation for a Nuclear Free Future. The US Smithsonian Institution has named her as one of the most influential women of the 20th century.

Now nearing her 80s, Helen is still outspoken on issues of nuclear energy. She feels that the threat of global warming is being used as an excuse to say, Nuclear power is the answer. No, she says, explaining that to fuel a nuclear power plant, millions of tons of uranium ore must be mined and enriched, and the resulting radioactive waste isolated, cooled and somehow stored away from contaminating the environment for half a million years. The process not only uses up massive amounts of fossil fuels, but nuclear power plants also exist alongside threats of meltdowns and epidemics. She finds it dishonest to call it a valid choice.

Helen lives in the US and hosts a radio show with the same name as one of her books and the subsequent film, *If you love this planet.*

Rachel Carson (1907–1964)

Rachel's book, *Silent Spring* (1962) is credited with launching the current global environmental movement. In *Silent Spring* and her other writings, Rachel challenged modern humans' quest for dominance over nature by chemicals, bombs, space travel and more.

Rachel had planned a career in marine biology but several deaths in the wider family brought financial responsibilities that ended her academic studies. Instead she began writing radio scripts for the US Bureau of Fisheries, supplementing her income by writing natural history articles. After fifteen years, she became Editor in chief of all publications for the US Fish and Wildlife Service. She was a born ecologist, long before that science was defined. Transforming her meticulous research into lyrical prose, she wrote three books that make an enthralling biography of the ocean; *Under the Sea-Wind* (1941); the prize-winning study of the ocean *The Sea Around Us*, (1952) that brought her two awards and two honorary doctorates, and *The Edge of the Sea* (1955). They became international best sellers, raised public consciousness of the environment and made Rachel the most trusted public voice of science in the US. These books, along with an Academy-award winning documentary film on her work enabled her to take up writing full-time.

During the 1960's, Rachel drew public attention to climate change, rising sea levels, melting Arctic glaciers, collapsing bird and animal populations and crumbling geological faults. She demanded to know how people would be kept informed about these challenges to the planet itself. In her book, *Silent Spring* she asked even harder questions: '*Whether humans have the right to control nature, to decide who lives or dies, to poison or to destroy non-human life.*'

Silent Spring became the handbook for all life forms on Earth by revealing all biological systems to be dynamically inter-related. Rachel became a social revolutionary by urging her readers to challenge authorities that were willing to destroy biological systems.

Rachel devoted all her remaining research and her next book to banning the widespread use of synthetic pesticides and environmental poisons, a concern of hers since the 1940s. Many pesticides were developed through military intervention in science after WW2 and a US moth eradication program that used DDT mixed with diesel provoked her far-reaching efforts.

She located scientists already documenting the worldwide physiological and environmental impact of pesticides and by 1960 had ample research on pesticides' destructive qualities. She called for new policies to protect human health and the environment, publicly challenging the practices of agricultural scientists and others. Her accompanying book progressed rapidly but her malignant breast cancer delayed publication.

The chemical industry and agricultural lobbyists seized the chance to threaten legal action against Rachel's publisher. However this galvanized the scientific community and the US public into demanding a reversal in national pesticide policy instead, leading to a nationwide ban on DDT and some other pesticides.

Alexandra David-Néel (1868–1969)

This Belgian-French explorer, Buddhist lama (teacher) and prolific author achieved notoriety for her daring journey to Lhasa, capital of Tibet and heart of Tibetan Buddhism, at a time when entry to Tibet was forbidden to all Westerners and especially to women.

In midwinter 1924 with her adopted son Lama Yongden, Alexandra journeyed secretly over the Trans-Himalayas, a mountain range parallel to the main Himalayan range, often disguised as a Chinese beggar woman and pilgrim. Unaware that British officials, believing her to be a spy, were also tracking and trying to intercept her, she eluded brigands and Lhasa guards, survived blizzards and other dangers, to enter Lhasa after four months of intense privation. The pair's more than thirty books about their experiences remain the most accurate and extensive source on Buddhist practices from this culture. *'My Journey to Lhasa, by the Western woman who entered the Forbidden City'* Alexandra's 1927 bestseller, guided many later explorers, some even claiming her experiences as their own.

Young Alexandra escaped her family home in Belgium to train as an opera singer. When her voice failed, she explored anarchism, feminism and Eastern philosophy before making a marriage of convenience with Philip Neel. In 1911 she left for India to study Buddhism and learn Sanskrit and Tibetan, leaving Philip to manage her considerable fortune. This money funded her travels as well as the research and study for her books.

The Gomchen of Lachen, Alexandra's first spiritual master named her Yéshé Tome, thus identifying her to Buddhist authorities throughout Asia. Later studies earned her recognition as a lamani (female lama). As the disciple of a Hermetic master, in a cave near the Tibetan border she also studied tantric Buddhist practices such as *tumo*, tantric breathing, which enabled her to survive the piercing cold and near-starvation of her journey.

Alexandra's close friends included Sidkeong Tulku, the reforming Maharajah of Sikkim. She also spent time with the Panchen Lama and other Buddhist authorities, finding them wise and civilized in contrast to British officers who evicted her from both Tibet and Sikkim. To reach Lhasa, Alexandra and Yongden instead travelled through China, avoiding warlords and brigands to reach Kum Bum monastery. For several years they rested, studied rare manuscripts and planned their next move. Their final tortuous, zigzag journey followed by two months in Lhasa is recorded in their books and supported by many other records.

Aged 55, Alexandra returned to India with Yongden and was widely feted for her success, to the chagrin of many younger, male explorers. The pair then settled in a villa at Digne in France that they named Samten Dzong (fortress of meditation). For 40 years, they wrote books ranging from adventure classics to *Secret Teachings in Tibetan Buddhist Sects.* They travelled and lectured widely, Alexandra in her lama's robes, Yongden in his black Western suit. After Yongden's death, Alexandra boldly renewed her passport at age 100. A 2012 film, *J'irai au pays des neiges* tells her story.

Chökyi Drönma (1422–1456)

After the death of her only child, Princess Chökyi Drönma at around age twenty renounced her royal position to follow tantric Buddhism. Tradition says she had to shave her head and feign insanity so that her husband and his family would take her devotional intentions seriously. She founded an extensive, powerful, and influential female spiritual lineage that became the first and most famous of its kind in Tibet. Samding Monastery, the Temple of Soaring Meditation that she established remains unique in having a woman as its leader with half the inhabitants nuns and half monks.

Chökyi Drönma, known as Samding Dorje Phagmo and also the Great Woman, was the fully ordained, spiritual heir of her Master and principal teacher, Bodong Panchen Chogley Namgyal. She was recognised as a Master in her own right and a contemporary of the first Dalai Lama who acknowledged her Master as one of his teachers.

At age three Chökyi Drönma could read and write, and valued education throughout her life.

She had a specific commitment to women, promoting Tibetan women's education, establishing nunneries, and creating roles for women in spiritual dances where men had traditionally played the female parts. She contributed to works of art, architecture, and engineering and influenced the development of printing in the period called the Tibetan Renaissance. One of the projects she sponsored was a series of iron chain suspension bridges throughout Tibet. Made of an alloy resistant to rust, some of these bridges still exist today.

The Great Woman's legendary powers so terrified one invading army that hearing of her anger towards them, they offered everything they had, including their plundered valuables, as gifts for her monastery and fled. Chökyi Drönma died at the age of thirty-four. Her biographer, a devoted monk of Samding Monastery, hinted that his writing had been heavily censored. He wrote of his grief that he could not acknowledge her as profoundly as he wished in male-dominated Tibetan Buddhism. Chökyi Drönma's story is explored in the book, *When a Woman Becomes a Religious Dynasty: The Samding Dorje Phagmo of Tibe*t, by Hildegard Diemberger (2014).

Controversy surrounds the appointment of the current and twelfth Dorje Phagmo who some claim to be in collaboration with the Chinese. Another Dorje Phagmo line is said to exist in Thimphu, Bhutan.

Shirin Ebadi (1947–)

Shirin has been listed as one of the 100 most powerful and influential women of all time. She is an Iranian lawyer, the first female judge in Iran, a human-rights peace activist and a 2003 Nobel Peace laureate, the first Iranian and the first Muslim woman to receive the award. This, plus her Legion d'Honneur medal and other awards, were stolen from her bank safety-deposit box and her bank account frozen, showing the forces against her in her own country. Shirin speaks out vigorously and repeatedly for women's freedom and for human rights for all. In international forums, she advocates against military attacks on Iran and is often in considerable danger from opponents of her pacifist views.

She has publicly reminded the US that although its policy toward Iran is couched in the language of promoting human rights, these rights are not served by US military attacks. She asks the Western world to spend its money funding education and ending corruption in Iran, rather attacking the country with guns and bombs.

Iran's state security forces have raided her private

law offices, arrested her staff and allowed her property to be vandalized. Shirin has been jailed for short periods and was once given a five-year prison term for 'disturbing public opinion.' The sentence was suspended.

Shirin earned her law degree at Tehran University, starting 'on the bench' in 1969 while continuing with her doctorate in private law studies. In 1975, she was appointed President of Bench 24 at Tehran's City Court, the same year that she married. Within four years, after the Islamic Revolution, women were forbidden to serve as judges and she had to resign. When she tried to open a private law practice instead, Shirin couldn't get her application for a lawyer's license approved until 1992, three years after Khomeini's death. While waiting, she taught human rights training courses at Tehran University.

Once she was able to return to law, Shirin worked on cases with a particular focus on women and children. As well as writing books and articles in support of human rights, Shirin founded the Iran Association for Support of Children's Rights in 1995 and the Human Rights Defense Center in 2001.

During a period of increased persecution in 2009, she was away from Iran travelling and has been in exile in the UK since then. From there she continues her commitment to peaceful resolution of conflict and to amending the gender-discrimination laws in

Iran's constitution.

'I sound like a dreamer, I know. The challenge facing us today is to think like dreamers but act in a pragmatic manner. Let us remember that many of humanity's accomplishments began as a dream.'

Marie-Louise von Franz (1915–1998)

From childhood, Marie-Louise was known for her formidable intellect, once disrupting a religious class so vehemently that the teaching priest insisted she needed extra lessons. After hearing her spirited arguments, he's said to have abandoned the priesthood.

At 18, Marie-Louise met Swiss psychiatrist and psychotherapist Carl Jung, then aged 58. He told her about his patient who lived on the moon and she responded that surely the woman acted 'as if' she lived on the moon. '*When Jung replied No, the woman did live on the moon, I went away thinking that either he was crazy or I was,*' she later recalled, '*I wasn't yet aware that to Jung, dreams were as 'real' as the world itself.*'

Jung next encountered Marie-Louise a year later, first as a student in his University classes, next as a research assistant, then as an associate. Soon Marie-Louise became his closest colleague, working with him for over 30 years until his death in 1961. In 1948 she co-founded the C. G. Jung Institute in Zurich with Jung and contributed to his major works, particularly the monumental studies on psychology and alchemy.

Along with their collegial writing, Marie-Louise translated for Jung using her doctorate in Greek and Latin and her later studies in Arabic. In return, Jung initially provided analysis sessions and training and eventually chose her as his successor.

Marie-Louise supported herself through university by giving private lessons and later writing her textbooks on fairy tales. *Problems of the Feminine in Fairytales* (1972) was followed by *An Introduction to the Interpretation of Fairytales* (1973) and *Shadow and Evil in Fairytales* (1974), all best sellers. During her rigorous research, she found numerous common themes and symbols in so many isolated cultures that she could not claim mere coincidence but rather evidence of Jung's theory of collective human unconscious. She became a celebrated analyst and the author of twenty books which made her a leading authority on the psychology of fairy tales.

Marie-Louise's regard for Jung and her love of the countryside prompted her to buy land near a forest, build a tower and live in it, just as Jung had done. There, without electricity and many other conveniences, she felt 'in tune with the spirit of nature' and wrote many of her books. She also travelled widely, lecturing in Europe, Asia and the Americas. The advice she gave to all her therapy pupils was as disconcerting as it was simple: '*Attend to your own psychic life, and hope for a synchronistic happening in your client's. In this way everything is kept open and alive, as you become the one unique individual you are meant to be.'*

Marie-Louise made a film series and also features in the 1986 documentary on Jung, *Matter of Heart*.

Margaret Heafield Hamilton (1936–)

Margaret with printouts of her code

In the 1960s, 24-year-old Margaret wasn't seen as a contender for developing the modern concept of computer software and designing software systems that would help men land safely on the moon. In post-war US, women weren't encouraged into high-powered technical work and this young mother with an undergraduate degree in mathematics got work as a computer programmer at MIT mainly to support her husband during his studies. But when the Apollo space program came along, Margaret rose rapidly within MIT and was soon leading this epic feat of engineering.

At that time, computer science and software engineering weren't disciplines; programmers learned on the job with hands-on experience. Margaret described her first days at MIT: '*When you came into this organization as a beginner, they assigned you a program which nobody was able to ever figure out or get to run. They gave it to me as well. The person who wrote it put all of his comments in Greek and Latin. I was the first one to get it to work.*' It was abilities like this that gained her the role as the lead developer for NASA's Apollo flight software.

As a working mother in the 1960s, Margaret was unusual, but as a spaceship programmer, she was downright radical. She brought her small daughter Lauren to the lab on weekends and evenings and while Lauren slept, Margaret programmed, creating routines for the world's first portable computer, the Apollo's command module computer. In 1965, she became responsible for the onboard flight software on the Apollo computers, an area that within three years had 400 people working on it.

After Lauren unexpectedly crashed the simulator while toying with the keyboard, Margaret sought to add code to prevent a real-time crash but NASA overruled her, saying their astronauts were too highly trained to do what her daughter had done. Undeterred, Margaret created a program note that eventually saved the first-ever manned orbit when an astronaut did crash it. Even then, it took Margaret and her team nine hours to restore the data and get Apollo 8 safely home. Minutes before the later Apollo 11 touched down on the Moon's Sea of Tranquility, its computer also started spitting out error messages. Earlier technical arguments won by Margaret and her colleagues enabled them to be understood and the situation could be rescued.

For Margaret, programming initially meant

punching holes in stacks of punch cards, processed overnight on a giant Honeywell mainframe computer that simulated the Apollo lander's work. Once the code was solid, it was sent to a group of expert women who threaded copper wires through magnetic rings. This was before RAM or disk drives; on Apollo, memory was literally hardwired and almost indestructible. Margaret's areas of expertise are too many to list here, as are the many awards she has been given.

Te Puea Herangi (1883–1952)

Honouring the injunction of her grandfather, King Tāwhiao that the people of Tainui must never again take up weapons to kill others, Te Puea, a Māori leader from New Zealand, stood firm with those Tainui men who didn't want to fight in WW1, especially in a war that 'was not theirs.' Government's immediate reaction was to conscript Māori men from the Tainui region.

As a young woman, Te Puea had already played a crucial role alongside three successive kings in re-establishing the Kingitanga (King movement) among the Tainui people. At the outbreak of WW1 in 1914, her leadership was of even greater importance. She brought all the Tainui men liable for conscription into a pa (fort) she had rebuilt to support them. A talented musician and performer, she composed anti-conscription waiata (chants) that were widely sung. When Tainui men were imprisoned and subjected to military punishments, she would travel and sit outside the camps where they could see her and sing to raise their spirits. As with other pacifists, Te Puea endured being publicly reviled for supporting non-violent ways of ending conflict.

At the end of the war, the 1918 influenza epidemic left a quarter of Tainui people dead. Te Puea placed 100 orphaned children from the lower Waikato area in the care of the remaining families. She then set out to find fresh land for her people near to their original tribal area before the land confiscations of the previous century. Ten acres were finally bought at Ngāruawahia, land to be named Turangawaewae, meaning 'A place to stand.'

Years of hard work for the tribe followed, draining and clearing the swampy scrub-covered area, building homes and raising funds to build a house for visitors along with a large carved house intended as a hospital. Waikato Māori also had to overcome the prejudice of local Europeans who tried to have them removed. In later years, Te Puea hosted several influential politicians and dignitaries which helped to restore status to the Kīngitanga movement.

She also focused on Māori economic and community revival and helped to address grievances over land confiscation. To her surprise and initial disquiet she was awarded the King George V Silver Jubilee Medal in 1935, followed by a Commander of the British Empire (CBE) award in 1937 for her 'personal efforts, self-sacrificing devotion and capacity for leadership in her dealings with Tainui, other tribes and with Pakeha Europeans.'

Emily Hobhouse (1860–1926)

After a life spent advocating for social justice, British activist Emily began openly campaigning against British-administered concentration camps during the Boer War. These camps incarcerating Boer women and children were built at the command of Kitchener, a British Army officer and colonial administrator. In 1900, Emily visited and reported on hundreds of women and children dying in these camps daily. At least 28,000 Boers are recorded as dying from starvation and disease, along with unknown numbers of Africans.

On her return to England from South Africa, Emily encountered hostile criticism from both the British government and the media for her revelations, but her campaign eventually influenced public opinion enough to get many of the surviving civilians released and supported, and many camps closed.

'The women are wonderful,' Emily wrote of the mothers in these camps. *'They cry very little and never complain. The very magnitude of their sufferings, their indignities, loss and anxiety seems to lift them beyond*

tears… only when it cuts afresh at them through their children do their feelings flash out.'

Emily returned to South Africa several times and set up many welfare institutions, then helped organise the International Women's Congress in the Hague in 1915, aimed at opposing WW1. She arranged the writing and publishing of the celebrated 1915 Open Christmas Letter signed by 100 women to the women of Germany and Austria. *'We all urge that peace be made…. we are yours in this sisterhood of sorrow.'* The published reply from a similar number of German and Austrian women sent equally warm greetings.

Emily's later fundraising efforts meant thousands of desperate women and children in central Europe were fed daily for more than a year after the war ended in 1918.

Using all her resources, Emily worked on for the welfare of women and children, rendering herself virtually homeless. Unknown to her, in 1921 a sum of £2,300 was raised in gratitude from the Afrikaner nation. In spite of her initial reluctance to accept it, that gift, made up mostly of small coins, enabled her to buy a house in Cornwall, the place of her birth, where she lived for five years until her death in London in 1926. There were no mourners or even a clergyman at her cremation, and her death went unreported in the Cornish press.

Her ashes were installed in a niche in the National

Women's Monument at Bloemfontein, South Africa where she had previously been awarded citizenship and is still honoured as a heroine.

Dolores Huerta (1930–)

Since her teenage years, this Mexican-American humanitarian labour leader and activist has worked for poor, migrant farm workers, opposing the racism, brutality, meagre wages and other forms of discrimination imposed on them for generations in the US. After many attempts to bring attention to their plight, in 1962 with César Chávez, Dolores co-founded what is now the United Farm Workers (UFW) and then worked to bring about the 1975 Agricultural Labor Relations Act, the first US law to recognize the rights of farm workers to bargain collectively.

Dolores still advocates for improved immigration and civil rights policies and better quality labour conditions and healthcare for all farm workers, especially Latino migrants. When she began her work in the 1960's, even hard-working farm laborers could afford only dirt floors in their hovels, no toilets were provided for field workers and sexual harassment by employers was rampant.

Her determination brought Dolores into direct conflict with many militant farmer groups fighting to retain their cheap and powerless labor force. Through her advocacy, she has been arrested at least twenty two times for non-violent civil disobedience and strikes, had her home vandalized and children terrorised and nearly lost her life twice. Beaten with batons while peacefully protesting against George W Bush, she suffered six broken ribs and a ruptured spleen.

Yet her tireless advocacy for women, children, the poor, and especially migrant farm workers has also brought Dolores countless honours, awards and medals and she has been listed amongst the world's greatest women. Following a lengthy recovery from some of her injuries, on one occasion she took leave from the union to focus on women's rights. She travelled for two years encouraging Latino women to make themselves available for public office. The campaign resulted in a significant increase in the number of women representatives at local, state and federal levels.

Dolores has given birth to eleven children, stands firm against men's attempts to appropriate her work and feels it is time for girls to accept that strong women are not unusual. Having been sidelined all her life because of her Hispanic origins, she grew up knowing that there were many aspects of modern society that needed to be changed.

In Diego Luna's 2014 film, *Cesar Chavez*, Dolores is portrayed by actress / activist Rosario Dawson.

Sofia Kovalevskaya (1850–1891)

Sofia, also known as Sonya Kovalesky, was an award-winning Russian-born mathematician responsible for important original contributions to analysis, partial differential equations and mechanics. The first woman to hold a full professorship in Northern Europe, Sofia was also one of the first women to edit a scientific journal.

Although her family included mathematicians, all her life Sofia fought male prejudice to work at her chosen profession. As a child, she spent days studying the walls of a room in her family's remote Russian estate which was papered with her father's old calculus texts. *'I passed whole hours before that mysterious wall, trying to find some order,'* she recalled.

Persuading her father to let her study in St Petersburg at 15, she startled her tutors by her facility with calculus but her father refused to allow her further study. Aged 19, Sofia responded by making an unwise marriage of convenience and moving to Heidelberg University where once again, she amazed her tutors. Despite recommendations from Heidelberg, because of her gender she was refused admittance to Berlin University even to listen to classes. Sofia persuaded the celebrated 'father of mathematical analysis', Professor Weierstrass, to give her private lessons and in time, surpassed most of his male students. After four rigorous years, in 1874 at age 24 she presented three papers as her doctoral dissertation to the University of Göttingen on partial differential equations, on the dynamics of Saturn's rings and on elliptic integrals and was awarded a doctorate, the first woman in Europe to hold one.

Despite volunteering to provide free lectures, Sofia still could not teach at the university because she was a woman. Her husband's mental instability worsened and not long after the unplanned birth of their only child, he committed suicide. Sofia cared for her daughter in St. Petersburg for some time before leaving her with her sister's family and securing a position as a *privat-docent* at Stockholm University in Sweden. In 1884 she took a five-year position as Professor without Chair and also became the editor of Acta Mathematica.

In 1888 she won the *Prix Bordin* of the French Academy of Science with work that so impressed the jury that they essentially doubled the prize money before discovering that the winner was a woman. About winning that prize, she said: '*Say what you know, do what you must, come what may.*'

Acknowledged at last, Sofia now called Sonya was

appointed Professorial Chair holder at Stockholm University. After colleagues lobbied on her behalf, she was also granted a Chair in the Russian Academy of Sciences, but never offered a Russian professorship.

Wangari Maathai (1940–2011)

In 1977 Wangari launched the Green Belt Movement to help reforest her beloved Kenya, knowing it would also help the nation's women. '*Kenyan women needed income and resources because theirs were being fast depleted, so we decided to teach them to plant trees and solve both problems together,*' she said. The Green Belt Movement has since planted more than 51 million more trees and given new skills and work to around 50,000 Kenyan women. In 2004, Wangari's efforts were acknowledged with a Nobel Peace Prize. She was the first black woman as well as the first environmentalist to receive the award.

The child of a tenant farmer, Wangari was raised in a Kikuyu village household where women were seldom valued and rarely educated. When she was eight her older brother persuaded their parents to send her to school. In 1960, Wangari earned a scholarship to attend college in the US where she gained a Masters Degree in Biological Sciences. After completing a Doctorate at the University of Nairobi, the first woman in East and Central Africa to gain this qualification, she was appointed chair of the

Department of Veterinary Anatomy and an associate professor in 1976 and 1977. In both cases, Wangari was the first woman in the region to attain such positions.

Wangari was an outspoken critic of the government that had brought about such social and environmental degradation in Kenya. She said, '*I started seeing the root causes, and one of those was mis-governance.*' After lobbying to bring about the fall of that government, in 1977 she earned a seat in parliament, was appointed Assistant Minister of the Environment, Natural Resources and Wildlife, and began the Green Belt Movement to remedy the devastating impacts of deforestation. She wrote four books: *The Green Belt Movement; Unbowed: A Memoir; The Challenge for Africa;* and *Replenishing the Earth*. A documentary film, *Taking Root: the Vision of Wangari Maathai* (2008) celebrates her life and work.

Like many activists, Wangari paid a high price for her actions. During her protests, she was beaten and arrested numerous times, leaving her with legal expenses that were hard to meet. Her Kenyan husband divorced her and took away their young children, claiming she was 'too educated and too difficult to control'. The Kenyan government invoked a colonial-era law prohibiting groups from meeting without a government license, extending this to tree planters. Various authorities used all their legal and military power to try and crush both Wangari and the

Green Belt Movement.

She was internationally acknowledged for her struggle for democracy, human rights and environmental conservation. Wangari often addressed the United Nations, spoke on behalf of women during the UN Earth Summit and served in many environmental groups. In 2009, the UN named her a UN Messenger of Peace. In 2010, she founded the Wangari Maathai Institute for Peace and Environmental Studies (WMI) to bring together both academic research and the Green Belt Movement approach to land restoration.

Lise Meitner (1878–1968)

In the 1990s, the records of the committee that awarded the 1944 Nobel Prize in Chemistry for nuclear fission were opened, revealing that Austrian nuclear physicist Lise's exclusion from the award was almost solely due to gender discrimination. In 1997, a flurry of honours, including naming chemical element 109 as meitnerium, were awarded to posthumously acknowledge this remarkable woman.

Girls in 1900's Vienna could not go to secondary school and Lise's parents engaged a private tutor, enabling her to qualify for the University of Vienna where she graduated in 1905 with a Doctorate in Physics, only the second German woman to gain a Doctorate.

Encouraged and supported by her family, Lise went next to the Friedrich-Wilhelms-Universität in Berlin where physicist Max Planck allowed only her, out of all the women applying, to attend his lectures. A year later, she became Planck's assistant, working closely with chemist Otto Hahn. In 1909 she presented two significant papers on her research on beta-radiation.

In the Radiochemistry department at Kaiser Wilhelm Institute, Lise continued working without salary, making many important discoveries in radioactivity and nuclear physics. At age 35, she was finally named Physics professor and made head of her department. This paid position was short-lived, as Nazi Germany's anti-Jewish laws rapidly forced Lise to flee to Sweden 'with only 10 marks in my purse,' she wrote.

Before her flight, Lise and Otto had led the small group of scientists that discovered the nuclear fission of uranium when it absorbed an extra neutron. Their findings published in early 1939 led to Albert Einstein hailing Lise as 'the German Marie Curie.'

In Sweden, Lise found work and also established a working relationship with Danish physicist Niels Bohr. She continued to correspond with Otto and other German scientists, especially her nephew Frisch and also assisted researchers at Cambridge University.

Letters now reveal that during correspondence with her nephew, Lise was the first to articulate a theory of how the nucleus of an atom could be split into smaller parts and also the first to realize that Einstein's equation, $E = mc^2$ explained the source of the tremendous releases of energy in nuclear fission, popularly described as the conversion of mass into energy.

Later in life, Lise received many awards and honors but the 1944 Nobel Prize in Chemistry for nuclear fission went exclusively to her colleague Otto. Her name wasn't even mentioned at the ceremony. Although awed by her discoveries, Lise remained a fervent opponent of the use of her research for what became known as the atomic bomb, a nuclear weapon. All her life, she deeply regretted her unwitting part in its creation.

He Ming Qing aka Kathleen Hall
(1896–1970)

The people of Quyang County in northeastern China, famous for their stone carvings, created one of their finest in 1996 to mark the centennial of the birth of He Ming Qing, their name for a New Zealander who gave more than forty years of her life to helping Chinese people. Erected in the same village where Kathleen established her medical clinic, it honours the woman named a hero by Rewi Alley, a woman who regularly walked the mountain tracks with her big yellow dog to visit those too sick or injured to move. '*She talked very fast, but she walked even faster … like flying,*' the villagers said of her.

Kathleen spent eleven years as a missionary nurse in China, studying the language, history and culture as well as managing a large nursing staff. On encountering the degrading living conditions of people in the Hebei mountains, she resigned her position as a senior hospital charge nurse and in 1934 gained permission to set up her own cottage hospital in the mountain village of Songjiazhuang.

Known by her Chinese name, He Ming Qing,

meaning clear and bright, Kathleen found herself not only caring for villagers but also caught up in the second Sino-Japanese war as Japan invaded China. She regularly smuggled medical supplies through Japanese lines to the Canadian surgeon in charge of the Chinese army medical services. She attended to wounded soldiers and partisans and recruited nurses for the army, often personally guiding them up rough terrain to the relative safety of the mountains. Kathleen also organised mule trains of medical supplies, getting them through Japanese check points and becoming a marked woman in the process.

In 1939, the Japanese launched a raid on Songjiazhuang that destroyed both the mission and her hospital. With difficulty Kathleen made her way to Peking to re-equip the hospital only to find the Japanese demanding her expulsion from China. Rather than compromise her colleagues' safety, she left for Hong Kong then secretly re-entered China with the Chinese Red Cross through Vietnam. Joining an army medical unit, she travelled north under conditions of great hardship and deprivation, eventually collapsing from exhaustion and beriberi. Sent back to New Zealand in 1941, she continued to promote relations with China, returning several times as an honoured guest.

The He Ming Qing Memorial Scholarship established by the New Zealand China Friendship

Society Inc. still provides three-year scholarships for Chinese women from poor rural areas, enabling them to complete nursing training in order to return to their villages and work for improved health standards.

Wilma Rudolph (1940–1994)

Wilma was a premature baby, the twentieth child of a housemaid and a railroad porter. As an infant she survived mumps, measles, pneumonia and scarlet fever, but severe polio when she was four left her unable to control the muscles in her left leg. Although doctors said she would never walk again, her mother taught everyone in the family to massage her leg. Four years later with her leg in an iron brace, Wilma played basketball with her brothers every day. Soon she could play barefoot.

In those racially segregated times, it was at an all black school that 1.8 metre tall Wilma set a new record for winning points in girls' basketball. Seeing her play, the Tennessee State track coach asked her school to form a girls' track team 'so one of the girls could be turned into a sprinter.' Wilma was that girl. She couldn't explain her speed. *'I don't know why I run so fast,'* she said. *'I just run.'*

During her high school senior year, aged 16 she won a bronze medal at the 1956 Olympics in Melbourne as the team's youngest member. She had barely travelled out of her state before. In 1958, she began college at Tennessee State University, the same year that this black college was awarded full university status. There were no sports scholarships for women and unlike the men, to stay on the Olympic team Wilma had to take on clerical work along with her studies, as well as keep up her training.

Confronting racism as well as sexism, Wilma took part in non-violent protests against racial segregation. In the midst of this, she set a world record in the 200-metre race, qualifying her for the 1960 Rome Olympics. There she won two gold medals before spraining her ankle badly. Regardless, she went on to help her team win another gold medal for the 400-metre relay race. At her insistence, after those Olympics her home town of Clarksville, Tennessee held its first-ever racially integrated event in her honour, to welcome her home. Wilma became known as the Black Gazelle, the fastest woman in the world, and received many honours and awards.

Three years later, Wilma graduated with an education degree and became a schoolteacher at age 23. She also coached women's track teams and helped many inner-city kids to improve their lives. She married, had three children and set up a Foundation to help young people, working as an inspirational speaker until her death. A 1977 TV film tells her story.

Many African-American women athletes such as Florence Griffith Joyner, the next woman to win three gold medals in one Olympics (1988), valued her help. Wilma commented, *'Every time Florence ran, I ran.'*

Sophia Scholl (1921–1943)

Sophia, known as Sophie was a German student and anti-Nazi political activist, still acknowledged as one of the most admired and respected women in German history.

Sophie was born in Forchtenberg where in 1942 her father Robert, the Mayor at that time, was imprisoned for making a critical remark about Hitler. Intelligent and well educated, Sophie was an avid reader with a well-developed faith in the basic dignity of every human being. After graduating, she worked as a kindergarten teacher until she had to spend six months with young children in an auxiliary war service. Appalled by the military-style regime imposed on the children, she took up the practice of passive resistance and in May 1942, enrolled at the Munich University to study biology and philosophy instead.

There a small group of students, learning of the outrages being committed by the Nazis, formed the White Rose movement, a non-violent resistance effort against Hitler and the Nazi party. Core members included Hans Scholl, Sophie's brother. Regardless of danger, they produced and distributed six anti-Nazi leaflets imploring Germans to passively resist the atrocities. Sophie was an invaluable member because as a woman, she was less likely to be randomly stopped by S.S. Military squadrons than the men.

On 18 February 1943, Sophie, Hans and others were arrested for distributing their sixth leaflet at Munich University. They had no doubt of the penalty they faced. Perhaps because of her gender and youth, Sophie was offered a reprieve from execution if she would withdraw her accusations against the Nazis but she refused.

At her trial in the People's Court, Sophie's impassioned and articulate pleas against war affected many men – but not enough. On 22 February 1943 she, Hans, and their friend Christoph Probst were found guilty of high treason and beheaded by guillotine within hours of this judgment. A 2005 film *Sophie Scholl – The Final Days* celebrates their stand.

Sophie is recorded as saying:

'Somebody, after all, had to make a start. What we wrote and said is also believed by many others. They just don't dare express themselves as we did.'

Irena Sendler (1910–2008)

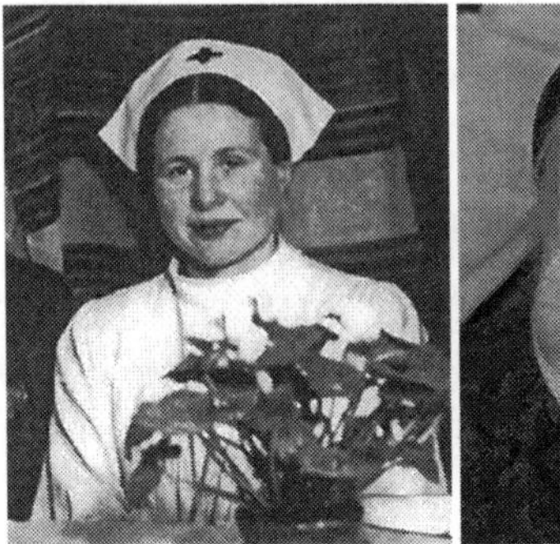

Irena as a young nurse and at 91

Irena, a Polish social worker and nurse, led a secret operation to successfully smuggle more than 2,500 Jewish children out of the Warsaw Ghetto during WWII, saving them from certain death. Working with an underground resistance movement, Irene's ruse was deceptively simple: to enter the ghetto as a nurse seeking signs of typhus and leave again with children hidden in ambulances, disguised as packages, or even tucked into sacks. The children were then given false identities and placed with Polish families or in orphanages. Irena recorded their names and new locations and buried the details in glass jars.

Irena began helping Jews in 1939, after the Germans invaded Poland. At first, she helped to create false documents for over 3,000 Jewish families and later joined Zegota, the underground Polish resistance organisation. Becoming head of Zegota's children's division in 1943, Irena used her special access to the Warsaw Ghetto, granted to Social Welfare Department employees to conduct inspections for typhus, to set up her smuggling operation. She and her colleagues secretly transported babies and children out of the Ghetto by hiding them in an ambulance with a false bottom or in baskets, coffins, and potato sacks. The children were given false identities and placed with Polish families or in orphanages. Although she was eventually detected, tortured, and sentenced to death, Irena bribed the German guards on her way to her execution and escaped.

For the rest of the war she lived in hiding with the help of the resistance, and survived to retrieve her buried glass jars. After the war, she worked to reunite the children with any remaining family members and restore to them their original identities.

Irena's story might be largely unknown in the West without the efforts of several Kansas high school students. In 1999, a teacher encouraged three of his students to work on a project for National History Day. Starting with a short newspaper clipping that mentioned Irena, the girls carried out a year long investigation into her life, wrote a play called *'Life in a Jar'* and in 2001, travelled to Poland to meet her. The play and the events that inspired it sparked worldwide interest. Many honours and acknowledgements followed, including a documentary film, Irena Sendler, *In the Name of Their Mothers* (2011) that won several awards.

Helen Sharman (1963–)

As the first British astronaut in 1991, Helen became an overnight sensation on her return from Mir, telling the world about her mission in space and spreading her inspirational story. She was just 27 years old when she blasted into orbit aboard a Soyuz rocket with two Russians, before spending eight days with them aboard Russia's Mir space station. Before heading out into space, she spent 18 months in intensive flight training in Star City, the popular name given to the Yuri Gagarin Cosmonaut Training Center in Moscow.

Helen was selected out of nearly 13,000 other British applicants in a rigorous process that gave weight to scientific, educational and aerospace background as well as the ability to learn a foreign language.

Known as Project Juno, the programme was a

cooperative arrangement between the Soviet Union and a group of British companies and Helen's tasks included medical and agricultural tests, photographing the British Isles, and participating in an unlicensed amateur radio hookup with British schoolchildren.

'I still dream about being on the space station with the feeling of being weightless, the most amazing, relaxing and natural feeling,' she said. Asked what she enjoyed most about her mission, she said 'It wasn't so much going into space that appealed, it was the sheer fun of doing science in space. Plus the training, a way out of the rat race. Also living in Russia, learning another language and doing advanced mechanics.' Asked about what appealed the least, she added, 'I'm a scientist, but have found myself being asked in interviews where I bought my clothes!'

Helen spent the years following her mission to Mir communicating science to the public. Her 1993 autobiography, *Seize the Moment: Autobiography of Britain's First Astronaut*, was followed in 1997 by a children's book, *The Space Place*. She has presented radio and television programmes including for BBC Schools and since 2015, been Operations Manager for the Department of Chemistry at Imperial College London and received numerous honours and awards.

In 2016, many people reacted angrily when British media mistakenly announced that Tim Peake was training to be Britain's first astronaut. Hasty corrections and public apologies had to be made, especially to Helen. She later gave Tim her treasured book, *Road to the Stars* by Yuri Gagarin to take with him into space. It had been a special gift to her from fellow cosmonauts in Star City. *'My crewmates all signed the book when we were together up at Mir space station and we gave it the official Mir stamp,'* Helen said.

Mitsu Tanaka (1945–)

Mitsu became perhaps the most visible individual figure in Japan's radical feminist movement during the 1960s and 70s, a tireless organiser helping to lead protests, co-founding the *Garuppu Tatakau Onnatachi* (Fighting Women Group) of activists and establishing the first women's centre and women's shelter in Japan. A key speaker at the 1970 Asian Women against Discrimination conference at Hosei University in Tokyo, Mitsu addressed over two thousand politically active women from all across Japan.

Yet despite these and many other efforts, the majority of the male-dominated media continued to mock these outspoken women. Japanese women got the vote only in 1946.

In response, Mitsu wrote her manifesto in just one night, calling for Japanese women to rise up and free themselves from male oppression. Her title translates as *Liberation from the Toilet*.

Why toilet? Mitsu explained that in Japanese, the word is a derogatory expression used by men to disdainfully describe women as little more than repositories of men's bodily fluids. *'In 1970's Japan, we were living the lives of women who didn't actually exist, and that anger spread through the female community,'* she wrote. *'The women's liberation movement in Japan was not about winning equal rights with men but addressing the fundamentally repressed roles that both women and men were forced to play.'*

One of the group's largest campaigns was to safeguard women's access to abortion procedures in Japan. The birth control pill was not legalized in Japan until 1999 and until then women had to rely heavily on abortion for birth control, although many regarded the process as repellent.

In 1972, Mitsu published her best-selling autobiography, *Inochi no Onna-tachie: Torimidashi uman ribu ron* (For My Spiritual Sisters: A Disorderly Theory of Women's Liberation), an account of her personal experiences with misogynist exploitation that included rape and extreme discrimination in employment. Mitsu and her role in the women's movement were captured in the 2012 book, *Scream from the Shadows: The Women's Liberation Movement in Japan* by Setsu Shigematsu.

Mitsu regrets that because Japanese feminists were not taken seriously by men, some adopted a masculine 'academic' approach and now use men's jargon in their efforts for liberation. She continues her work for women's health as an acupuncturist.

Early Women in Medicine

Lovisa Arberg

Women have always practiced medicine as midwives, surgeons, herbalists and more, with or without access to formal medical school training or recognised qualifications.

The earliest named woman in the history of medical science is an Egyptian, Merit Ptah, described in a 2700 BCE inscription as 'the chief physician'. Agnodike is recorded as a legally practicing female physician in Athens in 4th c. BCE.

Hildegard of Bingen (1098–1179) is considered Germany's first female physician and Dorothea Erxleben (1715–1762) the first German woman to be awarded a medical degree.

Trota, sometimes known as Trotula of Salerno, was an eminent physician and professor at the Italian *Scuola Medica Salernitana* around 11th century CE where she chose obstetrics as her field of study. Devoting herself to women and their medical needs, Trotula and others compiled 'The Diseases of Women', a 63-chapter compendium of medical information relevant to women's health, covering everything from anatomy and sex to menstruation and childbirth, in order to educate her male colleagues and students. For centuries it was a respected textbook in a number of countries. Another celebrated Italian physician was Dorotea Bucca, who held the chair of philosophy and medicine at the University of Bologna from 1390 for over forty more years.

A Scottish woman posed as a man, James Miranda Barry (179?–1865) to gain a medical education and practice medicine, and became a renowned military surgeon.

In Sweden, Lovisa Årberg (1801–1881) had no license for her practice as a doctor, as women were not allowed to study medicine at Swedish universities before 1870. When male doctors jealous of her popularity and success as both a doctor and surgeon laid formal charges against her, Lovisa was formally examined and found to have not only sufficient medical knowledge for her practice but also to be '*free from all forms of harmful practice.*' She was granted official permission to practice medicine and awarded a medal from King Oscar I of Sweden in 1852 in grateful recognition of her work.

Elizabeth Blackwell and Elizabeth Garrett Anderson of Britain struggled against the Victorian prejudices of their own cultures to become the first graduates from medical schools, Blackwell in the US in 1849 and Anderson in the UK in 1865.

Author's note – *Many more inspirational women, overflowing with the same fire that's in you, await your discovery. May you find those who speak to you, cherish them and burn even more brightly in their company. And may they light up your way in return.*

About the author – L P Hansen

The Fire Keeper's Girls burned itself deeply into the author as she pictured a community able to embrace the gifts that every girl brings with her at birth. This would be a real community, not fantasy, where girls are not family property to trade – or blank pages to be irrevocably etched with cultural demands. In this community, strong, unrestricted women already enjoy the best of themselves so girls can easily recognise where they belong.

But where are all these gloriously wild and wonderful women role models to be found, since the advent of the nuclear family and a society that selects which occupations and gender get the most recognition and reward? For now, some women must be borrowed – real women from other countries and other eras – and so *The Fire Keeper's Girls* began.

The book succeeds *Bad Oil and the Animals* (2016), a tale of teenage friends aiming a spotlight at illegal palm oil production and animal welfare in New Zealand and elsewhere, and *An Unexpected Hero* (2014), an adventure introducing New Zealand's WW1 Pacifist Archie Baxter to young readers. *Socks,* a story on homelessness, won the author the Jack Lasenby Senior Award for children's writing (2012).

Contact her through the publisher:
info@onepotopress.com

Made in the USA
Columbia, SC
05 December 2018